RED THE FIEND

Books by Gilbert Sorrentino:

POETRY

The Darkness Surrounds Us
Black and White
The Perfect Fiction
Corrosive Sublimate
A Dozen Oranges
Sulpiciae Elegidia: Elegiacs of Sulpicia
White Sail
The Orangery
Selected Poems 1958-1980

FICTON

The Sky Changes
Steelwork
Imaginative Qualities of Actual Things
Flawless Play Restored: The Masque of Fungo
Splendide-Hôtel
Mulligan Stew
Aberration of Starlight
Crystal Vision
Blue Pastoral
Odd Number
Rose Theater
Misterioso
Under the Shadow

CRITICISM

Something Said

RED

THE

FIEND

Gilbert Sorrentino

NEW YORK
FROMM INTERNATIONAL
PUBLISHING CORPORATION

Published in 1995 by Fromm International Publishing Corporation
560 Lexington Avenue, New York, New York 10022

Some chapters of this work have appeared in *Conjunctions*, to whose editor the author makes grateful acknowledgment.

Designed by C. Linda Dingler

Manufactured in the United States of America
Printed on acid-free recycled paper

First U.S. Edition 1995

Library of Congress Cataloging-in-Publication Data

Sorrentino, Gilbert.
    Red the Fiend / Gilbert Sorrentino.—1st U.S. ed.
        p.   cm.
    ISBN 0-88064-163-0 (cloth : acid-free) : $19.95
    I. Title.
PS3569.O7R43   1995
813' .54—dc20   94-32006
                                                                      CIP

5 4 3 2 1

My mother groan'd! my father wept.
Into the dangerous world I leapt:
Helpless, naked, piping loud;
Like a fiend hid in a cloud.
                    —WILLIAM BLAKE

Children and dead people have no souls.
                    —ROBERT MUSIL

O Jesus, behold our family prostrate before Thee.
                    —from "Consecration of the Family,"
                    MY SUNDAY MISSAL, 1938

RED THE FIEND

ONE

❖

Grandma smiles her malevolent smile, displaying both her gold tooth and her brownish-black tooth. She wonders, again, if someone might go down to the cellar storage bin and get her something.

She wants something.

Perhaps a hot-water bottle. An ice bag. A moth-eaten blanket. A chipped egg cup. Something personal, some treasure, something to bring back memories of her innocent girlhood, her winsome first days as a new bride. God knows, they didn't last long.

At the thought of the hot-water bottle, the ice bag, Red brightens internally, secretly, for such need may possibly signal pain somewhere in Grandma's body. He takes care to show nothing in his flat, brutal face. Pain that might foreshadow, perhaps, death itself, although Red does not even think this word.

Grandma says that it is out of the question for Grandpa to go because he's been working hard all day as he works hard every day to keep a roof over Red's and his tramp of a Mother's ungrateful heads. He has been working, today, like a nigger. That famous nigger!

And Grandma says, smiling, her teeth again defining the poles of death and artifice, that Red's *Mother* can't go. She's not finished doing the dishes yet and then she has to scrub the kitchen floor and then the bathroom from top to bottom. Somebody, God knows who, got it filthy today, just washing. Washing! How anybody can get a bathroom so filthy just washing his hands and face, and not a face to brag about either, is beyond Grandma. Grandpa nods, signaling that it's beyond him too. Grandpa has been famously working this day like the famous nigger.

Grandma looks at Red and has a sudden inspiration. *Red* can go down to the cellar and get the something that Grandma wants! But Red is afraid, so he says, of the storage bins, they are dark and haunted, monsters find themselves attracted to the weak lights that tenants use to illuminate their doings. They eat boys or parts of boys, and chew on their things. Red tells Grandma that he's afraid and Grandma looks as if she is about to have a heart attack, her eyelids flutter, her hand touches her sagging bosom, she looks wildly around the apartment, reaching shakily for the glass Grandpa has just refilled with beer, as if an explanation for this refusal may somehow be discovered, somewhere, for this confession of fear, this lack of respect. Grandma takes a swallow of beer and cracks a pretzel on her bottom front teeth, then suggests that Red cannot be afraid because he is not afraid of anything, *is* he? Wasn't he brazen enough to open Grandma's dresser drawer, her forbidden dresser drawer, so that he could look at a color postcard of the Budd Lake Casino? Her thin patent-leather belt taught him a lesson that day. Brazen, yes, brazen is the word, too brazen to cry.

Mother comes out of the kitchen and Red looks at her hopelessly. She looks at Grandma, who tells her that there's not enough beer left for her to have a glass, so she may as well start on the kitchen floor that her clumsy brazen son has marked up, out of spite, with his cheap black-rubber heels. Grandma shakes her head pityingly, and as if in wonder that anyone in the good old USA in the year 1940 could wear such cheap shoes. It's not as if they're wops. Mother's eyes are flat and dull.

Red suddenly stands up and says that he'll go down but he'd like to know what Grandma wants him to get. He talks loudly and with great confidence. Grandma smiles and holds out the key to the bin door's padlock. Her smile grows larger as she tells Red that he'll know just what she wants as soon as he sees it because if it were any plainer it would bite him. Red is a smart boy, stupid in school, but, God bless the mark, he can't help that, thanks to his shanty-Irish bum of a drunken Father. The boy can't help it!

As Red leaves, Grandma tells him not to take the flashlight because batteries are dear and money does not grow on trees but has to be earned by Grandpa who works like a coolie. Like a nigger and a coolie. Oh, Grandpa works.

There's a candle end in the bin and a box of matches. Red is to take care that he uses no more than one match. Money has to be sweated for by the nigger coolie. Who nods.

Deep in the rear of the bin, Red finds an old photograph album, its leather binding dry and powdery, covered with dust. Attached to it by a rubber band is a packet of photographs. He thinks for a moment, stiff with fright as he watches the weird shadows on the walls, feels his legs wobble, weak beneath him, and decides that this is what Grandma wants. He puts it under his arm and blows out the candle. His bowels feel dangerously loose.

Grandma is warmly astonished, and wipes her beery fingers on her greyly dirty housedress. The packet is exactly what she wanted! So, Red *can* overcome his stupidity whenever he puts his mind to it. Red beams and preens, thankful. He is about to explain his abstruse methods of reasoning, his methodical process of elimination, when Grandma laughs girlishly, one of her more horrifying laughs, and announces that since Red is afraid of nothing, it will be his permanent job to make all necessary trips to the bin. How does Red like that? Suddenly, Grandma stops laughing, her face darkens, shrivels, and she looks, amazed, at the packet of photographs. Then she says, as Red knows, as he has known all along that she will say, that these are the *wrong* photographs. There is nothing else for Red to do but take these *wrong* photographs back to the bin and look for the right photographs, no matter how long it takes. Grandma holds the *wrong* photographs out to Red, shaking them back and forth impatiently. Now.

A grotesque smile on his face, Red takes a step toward Grandma and completely loses control of his bowels. Beneath Grandma's incredulous and disgusted scowl is a faint expression of delight.

TWO

❖

Since Grandma knows that Red is conscienceless and thoroughly depraved, it falls to him to kill the mice that have been caught but not killed in the trap set in the cabinet beneath the kitchen sink. Grandma and Grandpa—and, halfheartedly, Red's Mother—know that he is as black as sin itself because of the terrible something that happened on the roof with that idiot daughter of the bohunk super of the adjoining building. Not that there's any bohunks with half a brain to begin with. But when a good Irish Catholic boy who's made his First Communion—and he looked almost presentable in the blue serge suit that Grandpa spent good money for, God help the poor man!—mortifies his grandparents, who took him in off the street and kept him and his Mother out of the poorhouse, and a lot of thanks they get for it!, *mortifies* them with his filthy sinful acts, it's not the idiot girl who can be blamed. Not that Grandma didn't drive Red's mother to tears scolding her to do the right thing and go over and talk to the unfortunate lump of a man about his slut of a daughter, a twelve-year-old tramp, idiot or not, and threaten him with the police if he can't keep an eye on her!

Grandma says, again, that that's all these bohunks and scowegians and greaseballs understand, a big Irish bruiser of a cop, not one, God help us, like Jimmy Kenny with his lard ass, to scare some decency into them and their disgusting families. Can't speak two words of English, any of them. Damn shame what this country's coming to. And Mother has to punish Red, too, does the woman, who can't even hold on to a man who was *halfway* decent when she married him, think that Grandma should always be the one to discipline the boy? Does Grandma have to do all the dirty work? She's had her child and raised her, much good it did her. She's got her cross to bear, although not many know it, for she never complains.

Had Mother put her foot down when the man started to come home drunk every night from work, and sometimes not come home at all, things might have been different. Now she's a divorced woman, a sinner in the eyes of the Church, not much better than the floozies who hang around with the book-makers in front of Gallagher's. And God only knows— Grandma gazes at the ceiling with an expression of fierce piety—God ... Only ... Knows ... *what* the truth of the matter is that drove the poor hardworking dumbbell of a man to drink. More there, Grandma says, a catch in her voice, than meets the eye. Grandpa nods and relights the cigarette butt he has already stubbed out twice. They're not made of money!

Red, the degenerate, the corrupt, the sinful, opens the door of the cabinet, from which have issued scraping and scratching noises. Behind a can of Drano is a half-dead mouse, his crushed, bloody snout and right front paw caught between the steel bar and wooden base of the trap. Grandma tells Red to do the job that she knows he loves to do, abnormal little mor-phodite that he is. And Grandma will not have Red flushing the mouse down the toilet! Drowning is the cruelest of deaths.

Grandpa adds that when you drown your lungs fill with

water and explode and you *feel everything*. The mouse is to be battered to death quickly, any way Red wishes. He is sure to think of something, since he loves such things, says Grandma.

Red picks up the trap and flings it on the floor. The mouse squeaks and its body twitches, but it does not die. Red throws the trap on the floor again, harder, and the mouse goes into convulsions. But it is still alive. Grandma remarks on Red's almost unbelievable cruelty, Grandpa shakes his head and leaves the room, Mother, anguished, looks at Red's flushed face. Red desperately throws the trap up to the ceiling and after it hits the floor this time, the mouse is still. Red pokes at the body with his foot and Grandma looks at Mother and rolls her eyes at this instance of sadism. She says that the mouse is to be disposed of, but *not* down the toilet as she does not want the filth and germs from the dead thing in her spotless bathroom that Mother just scrubbed this morning, does Red think that his Mother is a nigger maid? And, as usual, the trap is to be scrubbed with laundry soap, reset, and put back in the cabinet. And, Grandma smiles wisely, Red is not to eat any of the store cheese when he baits the trap.

Red, as depraved as always, rudely shakes the broken corpse onto a piece of newspaper and considers how remote the mouse seems now, and peaceful. He rolls the lucky little bastard up in the sheet of paper.

THREE

❖

Red looks at the icy stars through the front-room window from the vantage of the couch made up for him every night by Mother, and on which he has learned to sleep despite the sounds of the radio and conversation that come through the drapes. No one but Red is permitted in the front room, and he, only to sleep.

He wonders why God, Who made these stars, also made Grandma. Maybe He didn't make Grandma.

Maybe He didn't make the stars either. Maybe He didn't make anything.

Red feels evil doubt and black sin invade his soul and realizes that although he doesn't want to think these things, he thinks them, and that if he can't nullify them, Hell is waiting for him, just as it awaits all boys who mock God and have no respect for their parents. And their grandparents. To render the thoughts impotent, Red silently mouths one of his numerous magical litanies, one designed to expunge unbidden ideas. This particular one is based on the number 5.

Nothing. Nothing.
Nothing.

Nothing. Nothing.

Oh, may He take full possession of me forever.

Nothing. Nothing.

Nothing.

Nothing. Nothing.

May His divine Fear keep me from all evil.

Nothing. Jesus. Mary. Joseph. Nothing.

After Red clips off the "g" of the final "nothing" he squeezes his eyes closed, opens them, and looks again at the stars. As he stares, he says, again silently, that the stars that God has made in His wisdom are beautiful, but not as beautiful as heaven. Then, with his face beneath the covers, he whispers, as softly as he can, a devout prayer, repeated five times, that God bless and keep Grandma. Dear and good Grandma, who has her terrible cross to bear.

He thrusts his head into the cool darkness of the room, just in time to hear Grandma loose a thin, ragged fart, to which a period is put by her contemptuous laughter. Red's heart is filled with bitterness. He knows that he is damned to Hell.

FOUR

❖

In the dream there is a shape that is a woman at the end of the long hallway, a woman silhouetted against the light streaming in from the door open to the landing. Red is not permitted to see her face, but he knows, for certain, that the woman is Grandma. She is, suddenly, next to him, the door is closed, yet the hallway is filled with sunlight. Grandma is saying something that Red tries very hard to understand, although he knows that he is not really trying to understand, but that he is creating the words for her, shaping them, attempting to make them come together in a message that will carry Grandma's reasons for standing alone in the hallway, first as a shape, then as a faceless woman, for what Red knows has been a long time. Grandma says that she's pretty sure that they'll be playing ball today, that they'll be playing ball this afternoon, that she's pretty sure, Grandma says, that she knows that they'll be playing ball in Ebbets Field, that she's sure that they'll be playing ball today, this afternoon, and probably in Ebbets Field, she's certain. She puts her arm around Red's shoulders and he feels her freezing-cold body. Grandma says that they'll be playing ball today in the afternoon. Red says that it will be in Ebbets Field? She squeezes his shoulder, her hand a grapnel of ice. Grandma says that Grandpa wants Red to give him the Lucky Strikes, that he needs them to go to Ebbets Field. Her voice is Mother's voice now. Grandma says in Mother's voice that Grandpa wants his Lucky Strikes in time for the game and that she knows that Red is a good boy except when he talks back like a nigger monkey. Grandma walks into the kitchen to stare at Red's Father, who sits at the table, reading the paper and drinking from a chipped cup. Grandma looks at Red's Father for a moment, then turns to Red and beckons. She says that Red's Father is a hardworking bum who drinks like a fish. Red walks toward Grandma, who stands in the blinding light streaming into the long hallway from the door open to the landing. Red's Father is now behind her, smoking and smiling, and he holds up his cigarette and describes it to Grandma as a Lucky Strike. He moves it up and down in front of her face. Red knows that his Father is going to take him to Ebbets Field but that he can't go because he has to get Grandpa his Lucky Strikes, the Lucky Strikes that he wants. He says that he thinks his Father has Grandpa's cigarettes. His Father curses and shouts about begrudging a man everything, even his wife. The landing is dark. Grandma says in Mother's voice that the trunk will be here soon for Red's clothes and there will be another one to put Red in, the disobedient ungrateful pimp. Red starts to cry and watches Grandma slide and float down the dark hallway, past pictures of her that frighten Red, for in them, he can clearly see, she is showing her gold tooth in a grimace. She is sliding, she is floating. She is an unearthly white, wrinkled and shapeless and bulky. She has no head. She slides up to Red and he tells his Father that Grandma has no head, but his Father is gone. Grandma laughs coquettishly, and in a harsh voice tells Red that she has no head but that it will be here soon in the trunk. She presses against Red, she is soft and slippery and icy cold. Red looks at her and sees that Grandma is something else, some other thing. Grandma is her corset. She leans against him, she grows a little smaller, she starts to laugh. She calls out to Red's father at the kitchen table as if he is Grandpa and tells him that she's got the Lucky Strikes he wants. She surrounds Red. He is wearing Grandma.

FIVE

❖

Red eats ravenously virtually everything that Grandma sets before him. At those rare times, occasioned by whatever whim or aberration, when she offers him second helpings, he accepts, but warily, always suspicious of a hoax.

He consumes
head cheese boiled potatoes
fried chuck steak onions
waterlogged spare ribs sauerkraut navy beans
rubbery Jell-O
slumgullion
fried eggs with crunchy burned whites slimy yolks
liver bacon spinach
stale bread fried in bacon fat
elbow macaroni margarine brown mustard
green split-pea soup
ketchup mustard horseradish sandwiches
lima beans bologna
fish cakes Campbell's beans
tomatoes mayonnaise

tenderloin cabbage turnips
vegetable soup
frankfurters sweet potatoes lettuce
potato-and-onion stew
filet of flounder fried potatoes chili sauce
Woolworth's sugar cookies
soggy green beans
wax beans peas broccoli
and dozens of other foods, some unrecognizable, and including those of the invariable menus for Easter, Thanksgiving, Christmas, and New Year's Day.

But the one food that Red does not eat is kohlrabi, even though he chokes down its hated family members, cabbage, broccoli, cauliflower, and Brussels sprouts, But kohlrabi is scum and slime, snot and shit, piss, vomit, worms, and blood, all in diabolical partnership. Grandma cannot stand this willful rottenness, she blames Mother for spoiling the pathetic little maggot of a boy, God save him, letting him get away with murder while they're starving to death in Armenia and China and Arabia and who knows what other Godforsaken parts of the world full of hungry black niggers and jabbering chinamen that only Jesus Himself could love, what with them eating each other raw and their fifty wives apiece!

Grandma asks whether they think she buys kohlrabi for her own pleasure?

Don't they know, she asks, one hand on her weak chest and the other balled into a fist with which she hammers on Red's skull, *don't they*, that kohlrabi is cheap and full of vymins that the *News* says everybody needs or their blood will get thin as water and their eyes turn yellow like the poor afflicted lepers in Africa and their arms and legs together beJesus dropping off them as they walk down the street? Only the missionary priests, those sainted men, she says, only those sainted men will dare get near the disgusting creatures falling to pieces in public, God love them.

Grandma says that it's kohlrabi that keeps that from happening. She looks over at Grandpa and reminds him that he's a fine example for his scrawny grandson, and she glares at her husband's plate. Grandma looks up at the ceiling for succor and wonders why God put her on this earth to suffer a mollycoddle for a husband, a tramp for a daughter, and a savage Indian for a grandson, like his drunken Father.

But God in His wisdom knows just how heavy a cross each person can bear and He'll show Grandma mercy, oh yes, she's sure that He won't increase her burden, not one iota. He knows, she says, battering Red's cranium, that this is as much as she can tolerate. That she is only flesh and blood. That her tormentors take advantage of her kind nature.

Does anybody think, Grandma asks, that she buys kohlrabi for *her* pleasure?

Red stares at the kohlrabi growing cold on his plate. All then proceeds as usual. Grandma and Mother clear the table, the teapot is set to steep, dessert—lime Jell-O—is served. Grandma personally scrapes the plates into the garbage, but carefully slides Red's leftover kohlrabi onto a cracked saucer and puts it into the ice box. She smiles happily at Red, whose stomach churns. Whose eyes sting. He looks over at Grandpa who is reading a two-day-old *Journal-American* salvaged from the dumbwaiter. He looks at Mother, who is stirring milk into her tea. The long harangue, the protestations of grandmotherly martyrdom, the pounding of Red's skull, the flogging of his legs and buttocks and thighs with Grandma's thinnest leather belt—all are absent.

Grandma asks Red, in soft, seductive tones, caressing his face with greasy fingers, if he would like some more Jell-O, or a nice cookie? Perhaps he'd like some milk on his Jell-O? To all these questions, Red, head hanging morosely in the way that makes Grandma crimson with rage, answers in the negative. There is a deep silence, and Red looks up slowly to see Grandma glowering at him. Her eyes are bright with what he knows is a plan. Red slumps in his chair, *seeing* the nauseating saucerful of cold, gelatinous, greenish-white kohlrabi. It is waiting for him.

Maybe Mother will say something and Grandma will throw the kohlrabi out. He knows that this will not happen. Maybe the kohlrabi will disappear. Maybe Grandpa will put his foot down. Maybe the icebox will blow up or the whole house burn down. He knows that none of these things will happen. Maybe Grandma ... ? Maybe Grandma will ... ? Maybe she ... ? This will not happen. This couldn't happen. Red says Jesus Mary and Joseph five times. He considers that if he could become a leper maybe his mouth would fall off before morning.

SIX

❖

Grandpa, and then Mother, go rushing into the front room at Grandma's summoning cry. They stand, sniffing the air in disgust, appalled, and withal stunned under the barrage of Grandma's invective, oaths, prayers, and threats. Red stands in a corner of the room, partly protected by an easy chair covered with its customary white sheet. From the corner of his eye he can see out the window to the backyards and roofs of the sane and placid world.

Grandma shouts that they will be, they all will be, Red the degenerate leading the parade, they *all* will be satisfied only when she's cold in her pauper's grave, did ever a woman who means only to be charitable have to endure such an agony of torment? She claws distractedly at her filthy housedress, thus lifting it so that her run and tattered stockings, rolled and knotted almost flirtatiously above her sharp knees, are fully revealed. Grandma groans that the charity ward, where she'll surely end her days what with her weak chest and her nervous heart and her blood that's as thin as water, yes, the charity ward with the poor drooling ignorant hunkies and dagos will give her more peace than her own family, before the final blessed peace of the grave. She moves quickly toward Red and slaps him across the face and then again with the back of the same hand. Mother protests that there's no reason to hit Red in the face no matter what he's done, it can be cleaned up, she'll clean it up herself. Grandma looks at Mother with contempt and asks her if she can kindly tell them all when she's brought a penny into the house with her talk about what's to be done. Red looks out the window, his cheeks burning, his head ringing and buzzing, at someone flying a kite off a roof. He wonders if the kite might pull him right over the edge, the son of a bitch.

Grandma sniffs the air, beads of sweat on her forehead, her hands clenching and unclenching, and suddenly screams at Mother to smell the disgusting, sickening smell for the love of Jesus Christ, can it be possible that the stupid sloven of a woman is so far gone that she can't smell corruption? Grandma reminds her and Grandpa, who would like to get back to the Dodgers vs. Boston broadcast, that Catholic martyrs were tested for the strength of their faith in God with foul smells and stenches, yes, it's well known in the history of the Church, and by the Holy Family none of them could be fouler than this! She crosses herself.

In the center of the front-room floor is a large puddle of multicolored vomit, which is but a foot or so distant from an even larger puddle. Gobbets of partially digested food in a random splatter pattern radiate from the two puddles, and can be discovered on pieces of furniture, a floor lamp, a windowpane, three of the four walls, and even on the ceiling. They glisten moistly in the afternoon sunlight.

Grandma says wearily that the Devil himself is in Red, she can, she says, laying a hand on her heart, see the creature looking out at her from the boy's eyes. He's not natural. She says that those eyes want her dead, in her coffin; and adds that they'll all be happy to see her gone, buried, and if things go on as they have been, in potter's field. What with the two of them taking advantage of her generosity to eat her out of house and home! Or, God knows, maybe when she's dead they'll be miserable, for then they'll have nobody to torment any longer. At this reflection on her thankless role, she catches Red savagely by the hair and shakes his head back and forth wildly.

Mother cries out that Grandma should stop this, stop this, stop this, that she'll see to it that the boy cleans up the mess, that anybody can get sick, that he's only a little boy. Red feels as if his scalp is on fire and for a terrible moment thinks that he might vomit again, on Grandma.

The vomit is the product of Red's being told by Grandma that his breakfast oatmeal, which tasted sour and was unaccountably lumpy, had been improved by the addition of Red's leftover kohlrabi, chopped into small chunks before being dropped into the saucepan. At this information, Red left the table and walked into the dining room. He retched, then walked into the forbidden front room, his mind a dark mist, and there threw up prodigiously, trembling and shivering with terror and joy.

Grandma sits heavily on the couch, muttering that only a soul lost in sin would walk away from the bathroom to be sick, only a degenerate pimp of a scrawny runt from a thankless tramp and a bastard ne'er-do-well shanty drunk! She sighs, and her eyes roll back into her head. Anyone might justifiably be entitled to think that Grandma is about to have a seizure or to faint, except for Red, who is a connoisseur of her subtlest expressions. He knows that at this moment she is as alert and dangerous as ever. He asks the company at large if he should get a mop and bucket and Grandma produces a magnificent sob. Grandpa clasps his hands in front of him but makes no other move. Mother stretches her hand out to Red. Grandma whispers, as if to herself, that she never thought she'd live to see the bitter day when nobody would even have a kind word for her pain. She sobs again, her eyes narrowed.

SEVEN

❖

Grandma takes the charlotte russes out of their shiny white box and places each on a saucer. What a surprise for everyone! And people, *some* people, say that Grandma has a cold heart. That Grandma is not thoughtful. That Grandma pinches pennies.

She touches the crystal-and-diamond lavaliere that hangs glittering against the bosom of her black silk dress and says that they should know by now that she always tries to bring home a little treat on the days she has to go to the bank and talk to those sissified men with their airs.

Red notices, he can't help but notice that there are only three charlotte russes. He notices that Mother and Grandpa also notice. He notices that Grandma notices that he and Mother and Grandpa notice. He notices that Grandma puts on, first, her puzzled face, then, immediately following, her face of sudden understanding. Red knows that this is not a good sign.

It seems that Red, so Grandma says, sadly, will have to do without a charlotte russe *this time*, because of that bad tooth that's been bothering him. Sweet things are very very painful to bad teeth. As everyone knows.

Red is astonished at the news of his bad tooth, yet a moment later he is almost convinced of its reality. His bad tooth, his decayed tooth, his rotten tooth, his tooth that seethes and thuds with pain at the mere mention of sweets. Oh that tooth! Red grimaces and pokes around inside his mouth with his tongue.

Or:

(Italian creams from Loft's, poor Red, so subject to unsightly oozing pimples, acne, boils, even carbuncles. Vanilla-chocolate-strawberry ice cream from Arnold's, poor Red, the cold is so hard on his swollen and diseased adenoids, his clogged sinuses, his inflamed tonsils, his appendix, his nose, his ears, his eyes, his scalp, his tongue, his body, his entire body will suffer the agonies of the heathen damned if he takes but a spoonful of ice cream, it's a well-known fact. Hot chocolate is often unspeakably dangerous, as is lemonade. Coconut buns, cinnamon buns, crumb buns, all, on various occasions, threaten Red's health and well-being with hidden perils.)

Red continues drawing at the kitchen table, as Grandma, Grandpa, and Mother eat their charlotte russes in silence. He whistles breathily, then hums, then yawns nonchalantly before rising to go to the sink for a glass of water. He tells Grandma that he is going to be very careful about letting the water get too cold. Because of his bad tooth. He wonders if he's remembered to thank Grandma for being so thoughtful about his bad tooth, for protecting him from a charlotte russe. Because it would have been so easy for her to forget his bad tooth. He thanks Grandma in case he forgot to. Before.

(Thanks for no Italian creams, for no vanilla-chocolate-strawberry ice cream, for no hot chocolate or lemonade, for no coconut buns (ow!), cinnamon buns (oow!), crumb buns (ouch!).)

Grandma looks at Red darkly, pensively. His pinched, dull,

coarse face is blankly innocent. Grandma seems to be wondering if it is possible that the little imp actually *has* a bad tooth?
Can it be? It can't be! It would mean that ... Grandma scowls
and finishes the last morsel of her charlotte russe. Red drinks
his water and returns to the table. He sees Grandma smiling
curiously at him and he smiles back.

Red wonders if Grandma really *does* think he has a bad
tooth. She might. He feels a little ashamed and afraid that he
tried to tease her about the cold water. Maybe she cares about
his bad tooth?

Grandma says that he can skip dessert tonight too. It's better to be safe than sorry, especially since she's going to make
chocolate pudding. She tugs at one of Red's earlobes, not
really too hard, and says that you can't be too careful when it
comes to bad teeth. Red looks at her face. Now he knows.

EIGHT

❖

Red's wound is horrifying. It doesn't matter much how he got it, or where, or when, or what street riffraff he was with.

It's a ripped-open knee, pebbles, dirt, grease, and wood embedded in the bloody flesh; a deep puncture beneath the arm caused by a fall on a rusty picket; a purplish-blue knot on the forehead, its center a nucleus of black blood.

It doesn't matter what it is.

Mother says that Red might get lockjaw Mr. Bloom says. Mother says that she forgot to ask Mr. Bloom about blood poisoning but that she thinks blood poisoning and lockjaw are the same thing. Grandma says that Mr. Bloom thinks he knows everything but he's only a jew druggist, that's all he is.

A long ragged gash from buttock to the back of the knee, from doing something on a roof somewhere with God knows what dumb mick and dago scum of the earth Red calls his friends and where are those wonderful friends now?

Blood poisoning, infection, gangrene. Mother says that Mr. Bloom says that Red should see a doctor immediately to get a shot against tetniss and Grandma says that tetniss is not lockjaw but like the mumps and Mother says that Mr. Bloom says that lockjaw and tetniss are the same thing.

It doesn't matter.

What matters is that Red has got Grandpa so upset that he can't enjoy watching a softball game in the park. Grandma says the poor man is going to stay home because he can't enjoy a softball game what with Red and his carelessness and his lockjaw tetniss, the stupid clumsy horse's ass of a boy! Grandma says that she's God damned if the money she's giving Mother—and she points out that Mother is upset too, she looks at least ten years older since this morning—she will be good and God damned if the money she's handing over to some jew doctor for a tetniss lockjaw injection is going to be forgotten, not by a long shot!

Mother is sobbing and trying to comb her hair and put on a little lipstick and rouge, clutching some bills in her free hand. Blood is staining Red's shirt or his pants or his socks or his hair.

It doesn't matter.

Grandma says that it's all right for that rich sheeny, Bloom, and his sidekick with the little moustache that he thinks makes him look like Astor's pet horse, Fink, that's his name, it's all right for *them* to say that Mother should take the boy to the doctor, oh certainly, it's not their money that they're throwing away. She says that she wouldn't be a bit surprised if the doctor is Bloom's cousin by Jesus, you know the jews.

It doesn't matter.

A knocked-out tooth, a split lip, a lacerated ear, a splinter, blood and pus.

Grandma points out Grandpa's inability to enjoy a little ball of whiskey before supper what with the confusion and expense. She says that even if she doesn't show it the way some people do, shaking and crying and running to everyone for advice and begging for money that Grandpa works himself half to death for, even if she doesn't carry on like somebody gone crazy it doesn't mean that she's not upset. A stupid careless unthinking selfish gawm of a boy like Red doesn't care one iota about the hullabaloo he causes for the people who took him and his Mother in off the street when they had nowhere else to turn. That's because he's ungrateful.

Just by being there. Just by being alive.

It doesn't matter.

A crushed foot, a broken arm, a fractured skull, black eyes and abrasions and boils.

Grandma says that as God is her judge she doesn't think that there's anybody on the face of the earth who can cause more trouble than Red, he's so clumsy that he falls over his own feet. He's exactly like his Father that way, God bless us and save us!, the poor pitiful lummox of a rummy.

It doesn't matter.

NINE

❖

Red's Father has a new wife although Grandma says that if the buck-toothed Red Hook slut is his legal wife then *she's* Mrs. Rockefeller and besides he's still married in the eyes of God and always will be. Whenever this woman is brought up, Mother's eyes get wet and Grandma scolds her for giving a good damn about the unfortunate sot of a man and his red-haired tramp, Margie, is that her name? and a fine name it is too for a tramp. Margie or the tramp or whatever she is has a son about a year older than Red, a sly and sneaky boy named Terry. Whenever Red has to spend even a moment with Terry he daydreams about beating him up until Terry begs him to quit. But he rarely sees Terry and has even less to do with his mother because of the fit that Mother and Grandma have.

Grandma says that she got a look at Terry once and may God have mercy on us all, but he looked to her dumb enough to grow up to be a policeman. Dumber even than Red, who just might become a patch on a man's ass if he's halfway lucky.

One day, Red is on his way, with Bubbsy, Kicky, Little Mickey, and Franny, to throw rocks at the railroad dicks guarding the freights in the shunting yards that run along the edge of the park. His Father steps out the door of Pat's Tavern and calls him. The other boys continue on and Red goes over to his Father, whose eyes are red and bleary and whose unshaven face is swollen and bruised on one side. Red is embarrassed, angry, and shy, and he asks what his Father wants. Red's Father says that he knows that Red knows Terry, a hell of a kid, all boy, Terry Walsh, his lady friend's boy. His wife's. His wife's boy. Father looks uncomfortable.

Red feels nauseated as he looks past his Father and sees Terry sitting at one of the tables along the wall drinking a glass of ginger ale. Red steps back and is about to say something, but his Father half-pushes, half-pulls him into the saloon and sits him down across from Terry. The boys look at each other, Terry smiling guardedly and privately, Red frowning and pretending to study the lithographs of champion Irish Sweepstakes mounts that decorate the glaring walls.

There is a ginger ale for Red and another for Terry and a bowl of pretzels for both boys. Father has a tumbler of Green River with one ice cube in it and a short glass of beer. Red knows that he is very drunk, ossified, Grandma would say, because he is talking about Mother and what a saint she is and always was and always will be, that anybody can make a little mistake but that she's a cleanhearted, innocent girl as straight as a die and as pure as the snow. He says that Grandma is a tyrant of a witch of a woman without a single solitary generous bone in her entire body and that she was the one, she was the one who did it, oh yes, she spoiled it for all three of them. He says that Grandpa is a mollycoddle of a man who never got his hands dirty and is afraid to say a word to that woman who won't even let the man buy a pack of cigarettes every day and who skulks around like creeping Jesus with his God damn heart this and his God damn heart that, if Red will pardon his French.

Red's Father has persuaded Terry and Red to arm wrestle,

something that Red hates, as he hates all things athletic. He knows that he can't win. Surprisingly, though, he bests Terry after a considerable struggle.

Red's Father cheers exaggeratedly and drinks his whiskey, some of which runs down his chin onto his soiled Cities Service shirt. He says that Red is just like *he* is, and by fucking Christ, exactly the way his *father* was, God rest his soul!

Red and Terry join hands again, and again Red wins, this time quickly and cleanly and, Red knows, too easily. Red's Father says that they're to play once more, winner grand champ, and then Red better get home for supper. Dear Grandma might get mad and give him only three beans instead of four, the shameless old skinflint. He winks at Red and knocks his glass of beer over onto the table, already filthy with slops and ashes. Red's Father winks again. It is unspoken between them that at home Red never mentions accidentally meeting or talking with his Father.

Father says again that they can play one more time. He wonders if Red can make it three straight.

Terry puts his elbow on the table and his hand up in the air and smiles a cold, malicious smile. Red feels a chill pass across his shoulders. Terry says that since this is the last match because Red has to go home to his *mommy*, maybe they should make a bet this time? A bet, not really a bet, a bet to do something. To have to do something. Terry smiles and says that it should be a kind of a dare kind of thing.

Red's Father, who is trying to light a cigarette with beer-sodden matches, laughs and warns Terry not to get himself in a jam, Red certainly has his number! Terry says that he'll take a chance, he feels lucky.

Red looks at Terry and then at his Father.

He wishes that lightning would strike them both dead. That a great fire would fall like rain from the ceiling and burn them up like it burned up the boy, Sister Philomena said, who was reading the impure book, only smoking ashes were left in his bed and the sheets weren't even scorched. That they'd both die of a disease right now, their faces bloated, their tongues black and sticking out of their mouths.

Terry leans across the table and says that *this* idea might be good, listen. Red's Father's wet cigarette falls apart in his fingers. Red yawns as if carelessly as he flexes and stretches his right arm and asks, doomed, what idea?

TEN

❖

Red is on his way home from the Scotch bakery where he has been sent to buy fifteen cents' worth of day-old mince squares. Red loves mince squares and has an idea that he'd love them freshly baked even more. Perhaps one day he'll be able to discover if there is any truth to this notion. Then, too, Red—being Red—considers that by the time he has the chance to eat fresh mince squares he'll probably hate them. Red is beginning to understand that the world is a ruthlessly fair place in that it has no designs on or concerns for anyone, and responds, if it responds at all, to threats, cunning, and violence.

Red goes out of his way to see if anybody he knows is in the park or the lots, and as he walks beneath the peeling sycamores, he sees a bird fluttering amid the leaves. He stops, picks up a sharp stone, and throws it at the bird. For something to do. To add his little bit to the general cruelty. To be in touch with the spirit of the world. The stone hits the bird, there is a flurry, a choked, constricted sort of whistling chirp, and the bird falls onto the cobbled walk.

Red looks down at the bird and discovers that it is still alive, so he decides to kill it. As a matter of fact, it seems very much alive. One wing is grotesquely twisted, one leg cracked, and its black beady eyes are shining. Its plump grey body twitches irregularly.

Without a moment's hesitation, Red picks the bird up and, underhand, throws it up into the air. Red never hesitates when it comes to attacking animals and insects, for he knows that to kill things successfully they must not be given a chance to consider fleeing. The attack must insist on the ideal of destruction. The bird comes down and smacks against the cobbles. Red throws it up again, a little higher, and then again. And again.

The bird's head is broken, both of its wings horribly awry, its beak splintered. Yet its black eyes gleam and the bird lives.

But Red is merciless and throws the bird up overhand, almost to the top of the tree, then hears it crashing through the leaves as it plummets down to the path. Blood is leaking from its mouth now, and its breastbone is cracked. Still the bird's eyes shine.

Red thinks that this God damned fucking bird is still alive for Jesus Christ's sake! He picks up the dead thing and pitches it against the path with all his strength, then looks at the smashed, pulpy body, the louse-ridden feathers raggedly disheveled. Red sees that the eyes, although still gleaming faintly, have the dullness of death in them.

But Red believes that the bird is still alive and will be alive while it has its actual presence in the actual world. He picks it up and carries it to the gutter, then drops it down a sewer grating and licks his fingers. He thinks that it's good riddance to the stupid little son of a bitch. He is a little sick to his stomach, but he feels good. Completed. He feels as if he is, just for a moment, one with the vast entropic rhythms of the earth.

ELEVEN

❖

The boys are sitting in a circle on the sidewalk outside the rear entrance to Flynn's Bar and Grill. They are talking about pain, and how much of it they can stand, about games and how fast they can run, how well they can hide, about food and how much they can eat, what they like and what they hate.

Red says that even things that are disgusting and puky don't bother him. Blasé, he says that when he's hungry he'll eat anything.

Bubbsy says that he doesn't think that Red would eat a worm sandwich with pus on it, and the other boys agree. Red looks at them, his lumpy, beefy face registering a perfect ennui. He says, bored, that he's not falling for that kind of crap, they know what he means when he says he can eat anything. They know damn well that he means food, normal food, like people eat, no matter how lousy it is. Normal food.

A drunk staggers out of Flynn's, reels over to the gutter, and vomits copiously. All the boys think precisely the same thing, but no one speaks.

Red says that his Grandma makes head cheese that is so terrible the third or fourth time that even Frankenstein would get sick just looking at it, all dried out but still kind of slimy too. And cold. But Red says that he eats all his Grandma gives him and even takes a second and a third helping sometimes. And he eats and eats and eats till he can't move, if she lets him.

The drunk staggers back into Flynn's, his shoes and trouser cuffs splattered with vomit.

Red waits for somebody to ask what head cheese is, since it is precisely here that his prowess as a consumer of the inedible will stand wholly revealed. He leans back and looks appraisingly at a black Nash roadster across the street. Duck asks him, then, exactly what head cheese is, what is it, is it made out of cheese or out of heads, just what is it?

Red says that he's never seen all the things, he's never even been *allowed* to see all the things that his Grandma puts in it. But he knows that she puts in chopped tripe and lamb fat and chicken feet and leftover spuds and flat beer. And probably turkey skin to make the stuff bind together into a big like loaf that looks like brown Jell-O, like shit. With little specks of green stuff sort of floating around in it. Like weeds.

The boys are impressed. Bubbsy seems pained, Duck awed, Little Mickey slightly sickened. Red stretches and gets up and says that it's getting to be suppertime and he's starved. He's really *starved*. He smiles and says that he thinks head cheese is probably for supper.

At this moment, Big Mickey swaggers around the corner, spitting, as he does so, on the low step that leads up and into Flynn's front door. His thin, tough face is shadowed by the peak of his cap, and he sticks a Bull Durham handmade into his hard, sneering mouth. He carries a paper bag and as he sees the boys there is a slight, momentary flash of pleasure in his eyes. The boys are terrified. Big Mickey, whose true name is John McNamee, is a thief, bully, and sadist, who is as careless of others' well-being as he is of his own. Red considers, for an instant, bolting for home, knowing that he can outrun Big Mickey. But he knows that the next time he runs into Big Mickey, he will remember. Oh, he will remember all right!

Big Mickey stands in front of the boys who do their best to seem delighted to see him as they cower and gawk and laugh at his hateful remarks and contemptuous stares. In a terrible seizure of fear, Duck begins to ramble about Red's gastronomic achievements, his gustatory feats. He insists that Red can eat anything. Just anything! So Red himself says, yeah.

There is then fearsome silence, broken by the sounds of drunks arguing in Flynn's. In the air is the realization that this remark has put Red in jeopardy: the door has been opened for Big Mickey, who flashes his astonishingly white teeth and takes a last drag on his cigarette. He holds up his paper bag, opens the top, and gestures to Red to sit down. He says that Red should make himself comfortable. He says that Red should *relax*. Then he dumps out the bag.

At the boys' feet are some two dozen tiny crabs, boiled to a pale pink, and recognizable as the crabs that can be caught off the 69th Street pier with a string and a piece of spoiled meat. Nobody ever eats these crabs, whose bodies are each about the size of a fifty-cent piece. Nobody ever *cooks* these crabs. But Big Mickey has. The boys say nothing and stare at the crabs stupidly. Everybody knows they eat corpses and turds and scumbags.

Big Mickey pulls the peak of his cap lower and says to Red that he's waiting for him, the big eater, to tear into these delicious crabs, these dainties from the sea. God's blessed bounty. He pushes two or three of them toward Red with his heavy reform-school shoe and suggests that since they're so small, Red can eat them shells and all. Oh easy. He smiles and says that to waste not is to want not. Red is looking at the crabs which seem to be, horribly, alive, or partly alive. Some of them are still mostly blue-green in color.

Big Mickey tells Red that he's waiting, that he knows Red is no bullshit artist and that he hates anybody to bullshit him. He says that he really does hate it! It makes him mad. Red remembers Big Mickey stripping a kid in the lots, sticking a branch up his ass, and making him go home naked. He remembers Big Mickey chopping a kid's hair off down to the scalp with his fish knife. He remembers Big Mickey holding a kid off the roof edge of Warren's apartment house by his wrists. He remembers Big Mickey hitting a bohunk super around the corner with a brick right in the mouth. He remembers watching Big Mickey make a kid drink half the whiskey from a pint he'd stolen. He remembers Big Mickey stabbing a stray dog to death. He remembers Big Mickey doing something dirty to a girl and making her little brother watch. He knows that Big Mickey is a scourge, that he is a message.

Big Mickey is rolling another cigarette, his fingers deft, the sack of Bull Durham hanging from his mouth by its red string. He says that he expects Red to be enjoying his seafood, his fucking shore dinner, by the time he lights up. With a remarkably soft laugh, he kicks Red viciously in the shins for emphasis. Red picks up one of the crabs, the boys are goggling at him, Big Mickey snaps a match into flame against his thumbnail and smiles sweetly.

Red suspects, not for the first time, that there can't be a God. Not One who cares about Red. There's a God for Big Mickey, though, Grandma's.

TWELVE

❖

The desserts served at Grandma's table are such that Red dislikes them as much as he dislikes most of what Grandma sometimes calls entries. These desserts include Woolworth's sugar cookies which Grandma has Mother buy at the five-and-ten by what seems to Red to be the bushel; stale macaroons; stale Scotch shortbread; Jell-O, which after two days develops a thick, rubbery, rindlike surface; rice pudding and bread pudding, neither of which contains anything but the most negligible amounts of raisins, cinnamon, and sugar.

The sugar cookies, macaroons, and shortbread are made of sand, gravel, dirt, cement, pebbles, ashes, and ground glass. The Jell-O is but sweetened head cheese dressed up in garish colors—red, green, orange, and a gruesome pale yellow that is the color of piss. The rice pudding is, quite clearly, massed white cockroaches and the bread pudding some unearthly slime to which no name can be given.

On the rarest of occasions, Red voices what might be construed as negative opinions concerning one or the other of these desserts, especially as they grow older and staler. His remarks, no matter how mild, are always met by Grandma's warnings of destructive poverty and the poorhouse, tales of her destitute girlhood when she ate nothing but fried banana peels for a week, rehearsals of the heroic labors performed by Grandpa in order to earn the money to buy *any food at all*, oblique as well as blunt remarks on running a God damned charity for Mother and Red, suggestions as to what Red and Mother *might* be eating did they suddenly find themselves out on the street, God forbid, irrelevant asides on his shiftless Father and the slut of a bimbo he dares to pass off as his wife, may God have mercy on the son of a bitch, and addresses made directly to Jesus, or His Mother, or the Holy Family, imploring Them to look down upon and forgive ingratitude as bold as brass.

There is nothing for Red to do but eat dessert forever.

Unless he decides to give up dessert. All of it.

So it happens that one night at supper when Grandma is supervising the servings of lemon Jell-O that his Mother is spooning out from the shallow bowl in which the quivering horror is invariably stored, Red says that he doesn't want any dessert, thank you. Mother asks him if he's feeling well, if he has an upset stomach or a fever, and Red assures her that he's fine. Grandma says that he had better damn well be fine, she's never seen a boy Red's age sick so much of the time. The incident passes, and supper comes to its usual morose end, Grandma drinking tea from her saucer while she farts and reviles the neighbors, Grandpa reading whatever garbage-effluvious newspaper he's rescued from the dumbwaiter, Mother washing the dishes and scrubbing the kitchen, and Red struggling with incomprehensible homework.

The next night, Red refuses his ration of four Woolworth's cookies, and this time Mother feels his brow and presses him about his health, but again Red assures her that he's feeling fine. In a sudden dazzle of inspiration, he says that Sister Theodosia told the class that things that kids love—like *dessert*—can be sacrificed and offered up to God as an indulgence for the souls in Purgatory. Grandma, who is beginning to get annoyed with Red, who feels a frustrated, focusless anger, sucks on a tooth before saying that the nuns are liable to say anything, living as they do like a bunch of hens, and what in the name of God would they know about sacrifice, sitting down beJesus as they do to their roast beef and mashed potatoes and rich gravy and all manner of steaks and chops and whipped cream, and with the pure silk that they all wear, oh yes, next to their pelts? But Mother is smiling at Red, and Grandpa says that a little will power never hurt any boy. Grandma grumbles and stares so hard at Red that he can feel her eyes scorching the side of his head. He dares not look at her. That night, in bed, Red feels a thrill pass through his entire body. For a terrible moment he is afraid that he will shout with wicked laughter. His penis tingles and twitches erect. All is secret and silent.

Some nights later, Red still rigidly and humbly fasting his false religious fast, there miraculously appears on the table, along with the tea, an angel-food cake with chocolate icing. From Ebinger's! Grandma cuts three large pieces and serves herself, Grandpa, and Mother, while Red sips his tea, his face as dully beatific as his crude, smudgy features will allow. He is attempting to mimic the semi-moronic look that Mass-card art inflicts on Jesus. Nothing is said of this extraordinary dessert save for Grandma's remark that she just felt like a little treat would do them all good. The stupendous lie floats over the table, offering itself for silent examination before it fades. As Grandma eats, she looks at Red, but he is talking to Grandpa about the Dodgers' pitching staff. Grandma punctuates their conversation with lip-smacking and little grunts, and as she washes down the last bite of cake she notes happily that there is enough for tomorrow! Her gold tooth glows.

Red smiles, crosses himself, and asks to be excused. It is as if he is deaf! Grandma reddens and scolds Grandpa for smoking another cigarette that what with the price nowadays might as well be made of gold. Jesus Mary and Joseph!

The next day Grandma whips Red with her belt for getting a towel too wet. The day after she pinches his arms black and blue for not changing his shoes after school. The next day she boxes his ears until his head sings and buzzes for not washing his hands before supper like some kind of a black nigger. And the day after that she drums on his skull with her knuckles for getting a spot of ink on his white school shirt. There are many more manifestations of her irritability scattered throughout the next ten days or so: Red howls with pain, weeps real tears and brilliantly feigns shedding others, doubles over in agony and frustration, and has unbidden nocturnal visions of Grandma being eaten alive by stray hydrophobia-mad dogs. At supper, he continues to refuse dessert, making known to all that each evening his sacrifice earns three hundred days' indulgence for the poor suffering souls. He is by now adept at gazing modestly at the table as he speaks of his small act.

Grandma plays with her upper plate, yells at Grandpa, criticizes Mother's housework, and complains about the tea that they have the nerve to call Irish tea nowadays, she'll Irish tea the kraut nazi of a grocer!

Twice more Grandma serves surprising desserts; once a pineapple upside-down cake; once, fresh strawberries with whipped cream. Then she stops, muttering and grumbling icily for several weeks, sporadically whipping Red, smacking him in the face unexpectedly, insulting the unfortunate bullet head that he got from his imbecile of a Father, his flabby arms, his green chalky teeth, the wild shock of red straw that grows on a scalp covered all over with dandruff, his entire life and being, the poor little pimp.

These events begin to form Red's nascent understanding that the things and ideas which people love and covet can be exploited, devalued, wasted, and destroyed. In bed, he realizes that he has assumed some of Grandma's wisdom. It glows soft and warm in the dead center of his cold hatred.

THIRTEEN

❖

His boater angled rakishly, eyes in the dark shadow of its brim, his crisp ice-cream suit and white high-collared shirt strikingly set off by a dark tie and small stickpin, a young Grandpa leans against a tree and looks out at a world that has not yet set its iron heart against him.

This photograph of Grandpa fascinates and depresses Red. It almost always comes to mind at those times when Grandpa seems to exist as something less than human, as a kind of blurred cipher, a *thing* that Grandma treats with no more care than she does her faded and threadbare housedresses and her appallingly shredded stockings. The serious if somewhat bemused young man in distant sepia cannot really be, cannot really have been Grandpa.

He is Grandpa. Red knows that this dichotomy conceals some truth about life, or about Grandpa's life, but he has no idea what that truth may be. Whenever he compares the photographic image with Grandpa, the almost insubstantial present Grandpa, he gets dizzy and nervous, and he puts the photograph out of mind. For a long time, Red wonders how Grandma can treat Grandpa the way she does, for Red knows that Grandma has seen the photograph, has looked into that guileless, hopeful face. One day, Red realizes, so abruptly that it makes him momentarily blind, that Grandma not only knows the photograph, but that she knew Grandpa when he was that man.

The world seems to be wholly fake.

Does Grandma say to *that* young man that he should pull the *News* out of subway trash baskets, that he should keep an eye on that black Irish bartender at Carroll's he must have some jew in him to make sure he draws an honest pitcher of beer, that the reason he's still just a clerk at the insurance company after all these years is because he's got no gumption, that he should go and wallop Red's Father to make him support his lump of a son who'll eat them all out of house and home, that he *cannot* go to the office Christmas party, that he can't buy a new pair of spectators, that he's a sight to behold in his old highwater pants, that he never brings home enough extra soy sauce from the chinks' because he's lily-livered afraid that Wun Hung Lo will catch him, that he ought to get a little sun by the Blessed Virgin Mary he looks like a ghost or a mackerel's belly, that she's sure he's trying to make an impression on the new divorced tramp of a bimbo at work who's probably younger than his own daughter, that he's a mortification to God when he does his dog paddle at Breezy Point, that there's no reason for him to get his suits cleaned so often did he never hear of a good brushing and a pressing, that he looks like a bum with his shirts unstarched, that he looks like a snob with his starched collars, that he ought to be able to wear a white shirt more than once, that he ought to hang his head wearing a dirty shirt to business, that he must be trying to impress the boss that five hundred dollar millionaire shining his shoes with enough polish to supply a regiment, that he shouldn't belly-ache about indigestion when he goes around gubbymouthed without his teeth, that he should talk to that greaseball of a bookmaker on Gallagher's corner and tell him to keep his remarks to Mother to himself she's still married in the eyes of the Church, that he should stop smoking, that he shouldn't smoke too much, that he should smoke a pipe, that smoking clipped cigarettes is sure to give him a cough and she'll be God damned if she's to be kept awake with his hawking and spitting, that she knows he's been into the whiskey, that he's not to have a drink with Mr. Phillips the Protestant hail-fellow-well-met drunken wife-beater not that she doesn't deserve the back of any man's hand with her skirts so short and tight she ought to be arrested by the Legion of Decency, that he's not to be tipping his hat to nuns they're bad luck and always have been, that he should get a little exercise, that he shouldn't tire himself he's not getting any younger, that he ought to learn to enjoy a movie and come out of the Dark Ages for the love of God Almighty, that he ought to talk to Red about his disobedience and back talk as brazen as you please, that he ought to whip Red once in while and not leave it up to her, that he ought to smoke Wings or Twenty Grands but no it's got to be Lucky Strikes for Mr. Rockefeller, that he should sit, that he should stand, that he should crouch, crawl, kneel, lie, jump, fall down, get up, smile, frown, talk, eat, drink, fast, listen, look, stop, that he should live. That he should die:

Does she?

After dinner one Sunday Grandma says that she thinks she wants to smoke a cigarette! There's no reason why she shouldn't be up to the minute like the *ladies* in Grandpa's office and she just read in the paper that Eleanor Roosevelt smokes and holy sweet Mother of God if that woman with a face on her that could frighten the horses can smoke there's no reason she can't and don't the actresses in Hollywood all smoke till you can't see their painted faces with the cigarettes stuck in their gobs?

Red is utterly surprised at this request, this demand for a cigarette. He wisely puts on his blank face so that his blunted irregular features project a kind of semi-conscious indifference. Mother begins to clear the table and says that she's always been under the impression that Grandma thinks that smoking is for *those* women to which Grandma replies that she'll do well to keep a civil tongue in her head as the charity case that she is along with her son who ought to be made to close his mouth before he slobbers all over himself the poor dumb ox of a boy.

Grandpa's face is pale grey and Red instantly knows that Grandma, who permits Grandpa enough money to buy one pack of cigarettes every two days, Grandma is, oh yes, Grandma is suggesting that she wants to share, appropriate, take some of this, oh yes, some of this ration of Grandpa's small enjoyment. Grandpa once told Red that smoking is all he does now himself for himself.

Grandpa's face is paler grey now and Red, slicing a glance at Grandma, knows that she knows what Grandpa is thinking, for she smiles faintly. Mother, her mouth set, continues to clear the table. The kettle is on, and a chipped plate of macaroons, a Sunday ordeal, is on the table. Save for domestic clinkings and rattlings, the kitchen atmosphere is weirdly and silently thrilling. Mother pours the tea and sits.

Still nobody speaks. Then Grandpa reaches into his breast pocket, takes out his Luckies, and taps a clipped cigarette into his hand. His face grim, he half rises, leans across the table, and places next to Grandma's cup and saucer the half-smoked butt. Mother looks out the window. Red's face is the very essence of stupidity. He can virtually feel the heat of Grandma's rage and shock and when he looks vacantly at her he sees what must truly be the glare of death. Grandpa politely lays a book of matches next to the butt. He says that Grandma should be careful because, as she well knows, clipped cigarettes can cause the most terrible coughing. Terrible! There is a little color in his face now.

Red wants to jump up and scream and laugh and cry. He wants to shout at Grandma in her humiliation, so tangible now that Mother is flushed and looks helplessly bewildered.

But Red sits silently, his mouth slack, his eyes dull. He notices nothing. Dumb ox. Grandpa lights a cigarette with enormous care.

FOURTEEN

❖

At the end of a week of desultory, irritable conversations between Grandma and Mother, during which time Red's Father's name is brought up again and again, Red is told that his Father is going to take him out on the coming Saturday.

Red's Father is going to take him out?

Red greets this news with a nervous passivity that permits no emotion to show. He has no clear idea what emotion is properly called for, and knows that to make a mistake can open the way to sustained misery, one that can function according to permutations as elaborate as those of a fugue. Grandma says that you might as well talk to the wall as try and get a word out of Red. She is more convinced than ever that the boy must have a little mongolian idiot in him. Mother asks Red if he doesn't think it's nice that his Father will be taking him out and Red says that it's nice. Real nice. He keeps his voice flat and toneless. No use taking a chance with anything. Grandma shakes her head and says that Red and his Father make a pretty pair of dumbbells.

Red almost immediately forgets about the coming Saturday. He suspects that the future is something that but rarely enters in the guise predicted for it, that to step into the ice-cream parlor is to find that you've lost your nickel. Red fulfills the requirements of his life by living it as gingerly and tentatively as possible, in the hope that it might pass by without noticing him.

Red's Father is sweating furiously long before they reach the Coney Island Stillwell Avenue station, and he smells sweet, with a suggestion of slow decay at the bottom of the sweetness. Red knows that he is mammothly hung over and needs a drink, and so he is not surprised when, after reaching the Boardwalk, they stop into a breezy saloon, whose front is completely open to the Boardwalk, beach, and sea. Red's Father has a double Three Feathers and a draft beer and Red an orange soda. His Father's voice is variously addressed to the bartender and to him, but Red arranges his hearing so that his Father's words become one with the hum and clatter of the summery world at large. It is one of Red's most common defensive tactics. His Father is probably going to become so paralyzed that Red will have to clean the vomit off him and then get him onto the subway and maybe even take him home to his bimbo wife. This prospect doesn't disappoint or even anger Red, or so he thinks. He permits himself few expectations and always expects the worst.

Yet his Father remains reasonably sober, or as he might say, mellow, drinking just enough to keep from being sick, or from getting the shakes, or from having the horrors. Red pictures the horrors as little flame-red people in housedresses who sit on his Father's shoulders and repeatedly stab him in the eyes and ears with razor-sharp daggers.

They go on the carrousel, the whip, and the bumping cars, where Red's Father embarrasses him by running into, four times, two girls who laugh and scream and smile at Father. Red knows that they're just a couple of guinea tramps. The world is full of tramps. And bums and sluts and bimbos and hooers. Red knows this. Red's Father is so excited after he talks to the tramps when the ride ends that Red wishes he *would* get paralyzed. For Christ's sake! Red can hardly stand him, his red sweaty face, his crooked teeth, his Mother *did* whatever they do with this man?

Late in the afternoon, the breeze sweeping in from the ocean cool now, the impossible occurs in a penny arcade. Red's Father, after putting more than two dollars' worth of pennies into a machine, does that which nobody can really do. The machine, a glass box half-filled with red candy beans among which are scattered various prizes, deploys a miniature crane to which is attached, by a cable, a metal basket whose toothed jaws open and close according to the player's manipulations— one penny permits the player one complete series of crane-cable-basket movements. The basket hangs suspended above the garish drifts of candy beans amid which Red can see a comb, a whistle, a small top, a pocket mirror, a mechanical pencil, and a table lighter. A large, smooth, glistening table lighter, one that is just slightly smaller than the basket's open jaws. Nobody can capture the lighter, it is there merely to make people—dumb people like his drunk Father—spend all their money for a handful of shitty candy. That's all.

Red's Father, with the calm, almost elegant intensity of someone who doesn't know that he must lose, shakes the rigid laws that govern losers and the very art of losing, and the lighter tumbles into the chute. And then down and out and into Red's Father's hands. Red grasps his Father's wrist, looks into his sweating, ecstatic face, Jesus Christ, Jesus, Jesus Christ. His Father puts the lighter into Red's hands and squeezes his shoulders. They stop off at Nathan's where Red eats hot dogs and his Father drinks a few beers. Two beaming fools.

From the moment Red walks into the apartment that evening with the glorious lighter in his hand, held out for all to see, the lighter intended as a present for Grandpa, from that moment when he makes the unbelievable mistake of speaking of his Father's feat, the lighter ceases to exist as an actual object.

The lighter sits on an end table in the dining room, the table next to the Morris chair whose arm Grandma likes to throw her leg over, blithely, so as to expose herself stupidly and all unawares. The lighter needs a flint and fuel. It will need a flint and fuel forever. For the first month of the lighter's eerie and useless presence, Red idly twirls its strike wheel, opens the screw cap on its base and looks at the dry, pristine cotton visible, hefts the smooth, heavy, gleaming chrome barrel in his hand. As he performs these rote acts, acts which daily grow more hopeless, pathetic, and unreal, he begins to understand that the lighter does not truly exist. He asks Grandpa when he'll fix the lighter up. So he can have a lighter all the time. Grandpa looks trapped and says that a cheap lighter can explode in your hand. You've got to be careful with cheap lighters.

So the lighter daily sits in its place, dusted faithfully but with an air of disgust by his Mother. Treason. It speaks of Red's unforgivable treason. He has dreams of lightning flashing from the lighter, of giant flames roaring, burning everything in the apartment, burning it all to nothing.

FIFTEEN

❖

Grandma never goes to Mass. The cold marble smell of the church and its lingering incense fills her with panic, as does the sight of the celebrant priests and their altar boys. She is, nonetheless, always involved with Red's preparations for church.

Red's blue serge knickers have a tear, not yet mended by Mother, in one of the knees, damage for which Red has already paid with a desultory cuff to the face from Mother and several serious whacks on the buttocks with a wooden hanger from Grandma. He thinks they're made of money. Grandma says that he's not fit to be seen in those pants on a Sunday and Mother agrees. He looks like some ragamuffin on the home relief. So Red is told to wear his blue serge shorts and long white cotton stockings. Red hates this outfit. Only little kids, kindergarten kids, wear long stockings—and *girls*—stockings that are attached to humiliating garters sewn into the legs of the shorts. He says that he can wear short socks, that he *will* wear short socks, he's not a baby and he's not a girl.

Mother swats him across the head a couple of times with the rotogravure section of the *News*, and Grandma sharply pokes a finger into his ribs to convince him of his error. She says that she has a mind to let him catch his death of cold but then who will have to take him to the hospital and pay the bills? Who? Of course!

If Fredo sees Red on the street he'll knock him flat on his ass.

Red says that the blue-and-white-striped tie is choking him it's so tight, and can't he just wear the red clip-on tie that Mr. Svensen gave him for Christmas? He begins to loosen the tie, coughing and gasping assiduously.

Mother slaps him rather desperately across the face one way and then, with the back of her hand, the other way, and Grandma nods contentedly as she pinches the skin of Red's forearm just below the crook of his elbow. Her nails draw a little blood, just a little. She says that the red tie is a sure sign if ever one were needed that Mr. Svensen has his brains hid in his ass like the rest of the Swedes. They're always soused, anyway, as everyone knows. Mother adds that red ties are what the Communists wear.

If Fredo sees Red on the street he will kick the sweet beJesus out of him.

Red says that he hates to wear that green gooey stuff in his hair, it makes it greasy and stiff, and it smells like perfume. He's decided to just wet his hair with water, that's all, just wet it down with a little water.

Mother grabs a handful of Red's hair and pours the syrupy lime-green liquid on his head, then combs the tangles and knots into a glistening red helmet, while Grandma tightens the knot of his tie a little more and says that she doesn't want to see it loose when he comes home or he'll rue the day.

If Fredo sees Red on the street he'll bang him over the head with a garbage-can lid.

Red leaves the house, walks to the corner, and then quickly

heads for the park. As soon as he enters, he veers off the deserted path and walks across the grass to a clump of shrubs. He looks around carefully and steps behind them. He pulls off his tie, and puts it, knotted, into his jacket pocket, ungarters his stockings and rolls them to just above his ankles, and pulls off and puts on his knitted nooby five or six times, until the brittle surface of his hair is somewhat softer. Then he returns to the path and trudges down it to the first tunnel. He lifts up a loose cobblestone just inside the tunnel entrance and from a little depression dug in the soil beneath, pulls a half-pack of Wings and a book of matches wrapped in layers of oilcloth, newspaper, and brown butcher paper. He reclines on the sere, cold grass and has a smoke. He knows that he is committing a mortal sin by skipping Mass, and he knows that he will commit another mortal sin by not confessing it.

He feels very good.

Sin! Sin!

Red smokes another delicious cigarette, rearranges his cache carefully, places the stone on top, and then walks up a small rise, under a sparse copse of crabapple trees, and onto the street. He walks slowly around the block, strolls over to check the clock in the gas station, and sees that it's five to ten. Perfect. He stands behind a car, puts on his tie and knots it tight, pulls up his stockings and garters them, checks his hair to see that it seems naturally mussed. All right.

He enters the apartment to the smell of roast leg of lamb. Grandma steps out of the kitchen and looks him up and down as he walks toward her down the long hallway. She bars his way to the dining room, her face beginning to darken angrily with blood, as she stares at his face and then at his feet. Shaking her head sadly, she asks him why his shoes, his Sunday shoes that cost a king's ransom at Thom McAn, are caked and by Christ *covered* with mud and grass. She asks him why. She asks him why. She asks him where. She asks him *why*. She wonders what has happened to Our Lady of Angels, what has happened, she wonders, to its floor, she wonders if they say Mass in a barn now, like the Albanians. She asks him.

Red's mind opens, rather peacefully, onto an interior white space that is suddenly filled with a pain that enters through his left ear, ringing and clanging with the solid blow delivered to it by a wooden potato masher.

He says that it must have rained? Last night? He says that Sister Margaret Mary said she liked his tie. All his sad flags are flying.

SIXTEEN

❖

Mother and Mrs. O'Neill take Red and Nancy to the beach at Coney Island. They settle on their blankets in front of Scoville's, where a lot of the American people from the neighborhood go, and there are no jews. Let them have the rest of Coney Island, a beautiful place once that they've completely ruined. Mother says that when she was a girl Coney Island was a paradise fit for a king. Mrs. O'Neill nods her head sadly and tells a story about some jews eating pieces of Christian babies raw under the boardwalk over near Brighton. They hushed it up, the jew newspapers.

Nancy, who is a practiced whiner, stays on the blanket with the two women while Red goes in the water; for Red, this is just as well. If he splashes her, if a wave knocks her down, if she swallows some water, Red knows that she'll manage to blame him. On the other hand, the last time they were at the beach together, Red managed to put his hand in between her legs as if accidentally. On her twat.

Red splashes around and pretends to swim, he plunges his head under, falls into oncoming waves, fills his mouth with water and spits it out in streams, in sprays, in gouts. He begins to shiver and turn blue. When he finally comes out, teeth chattering, Mother gives him a towel to drape over his shoulders and tells him not to go back in the water till he's warmed through, he can get a chill and die or get a cramp and die or his eyeballs can dry up and pop. He's to be good and stay on the blanket with Nancy. Mrs. O'Neill tells Nancy she's to be good and stay on the blanket with Red. The women are going in for a dip. Red watches them walk slowly into the water until it's up to their waists, then face each other and continue talking, probably still about how Phil the butcher's chuck chopped from the tray can't be trusted, it's all fat.

Red asks Nancy why she doesn't go in for a swim and she tells him to mind his own business, that he's ugly and too stupid even to talk to. She knows that he's being promoted into 6A-4, the dumbbell class with the morons and morphodites and the bad kids who shoot crap and smoke and talk about dirty things, like the Rongo brothers and the other filthy wops. Red blushes and says that she's a hooer and that her garbage-man father is not really her father but some dumb polack her mother met in Pat's Tavern. Everybody knows that her mother nagged her real father into Kings County and then to his grave. Nancy starts to cry and Red says that if she's still crying when their mothers get back he'll tell his Mother that she called *his* Father a skirt-chasing bum and that he couldn't help it but he hit her a little. She'd better shut the hell up or he'll hit her anyway. Nancy stops crying and says that she doesn't care because Red will go to Hell with the Protestants because of what he did with the super's daughter up on the roof. Everybody knows. Red blushes again and says that the super's daughter is a hooer and besides she can't even speak English. Nancy only smiles. She says that she thinks it's time for a dip in such a way as to make him want to slap her right in her dim freckled face or maybe hit her in her dumb twat.

Nancy minces down to the water and tiptoes in, crossing her arms over her chest. Mrs. O'Neill yells at her and then slaps her bare thighs a couple of times. That hurts! The three start back to the blanket together. Nancy was not to leave the blanket! Red and she were supposed to guard the clothes and change purses and whatever other treasures there are to tempt the dozens of tireless thieves who tirelessly roam the beach. By the score, the hundreds, the thousands.

Kikes and guineas. Gypsies!

Nancy is biting her lip and her eyes are red and swollen and brimming over with tears. Red feels a little sorry for her, but the main thing is that *he's* not being blamed! Better Nancy than Red. Soon they pack up and head for the subway.

Red and Mother arrive home in plenty of time for supper. They are hot and sweaty and sandy. After they shower, rare, wondrous showers which Grandma says make the bathroom look as if a herd of truck horses passed through, Grandma puts down the *New York World* and looks over her glasses at them. She says that:

people go to the beach to cool off and come back hot and filthy and sweaty worse off than before they left damn fools

the beach is for horses' asses and people who want to get black as niggers she can't understand it

she hears that there are a lot of niggers at Coney Island nowadays along with the kikes and the guineas it's not what it was when she was a girl when the women strolled along the boardwalk with their picture hats and white gloves and parasols it was a paradise fit for a king

it used to be a place for decent people to spend a summer day and evening not the riffraff and the dese dems and dose that you find nowadays

Francis X. Bushman Weber and Fields Al Jolson Eddie Cantor Fanny Brice Charlie Chaplin the King of England Rudolph

Valentino the Crown Prince of Transylvania Kid McCoy Pope
Pius Lillian Russell Diamond Jim Brady Vernon and Irene Cas-
tle Harry Langdon Theda Bara Black Jack Pershing Alexan-
der's Ragtime Band featuring John Philip Sousa playing a
famous sort-of-various violin they were all oh yes Coney
Island regulars and they loved every minute of it and nothing
snooty about them either they often bathed all together good
clean fun it was

    they used to bottle the ocean water to send to poor bohunks
in the coal mines of Scranton and whatever other Godforsaken
places to cure their children of the scabies and the lice that ate
them alive

    you take your life in your hands now if you spend too much
time in the water

    infantile paralysis

    styes

    consumption

    warts

    pink eye

    poison blood

    mastoids

    worms some of them a foot long

    if some poor dimwit is crazy enough to get any of that
water that used to be so pure you could season your corn on
the cob with it at the clambakes that the decent people had in
Breezy Point well Breezy Point is still nice they have the brains
to keep it restricted that water is now so filthy with God
knows what filth those people even at Scoville's do in it if he
should get it in his mouth or swallow it God help him

    by God it looks like a sewer at some of those beaches espe-
cially near Nathan's where the scum of the earth congregate
with their sour cream and herring and ickle-mickle-dickle talk

    there are things in that water that a lady doesn't even want to mention the name of but they're alive crawling with germs and diseases they'll rot the skin off you in a week and you can kiss a good Catholic marriage with a good Catholic girl good-bye

your gums and tongue and the roof of your mouth can swell up like balloons overnight and by the Sacred Blood of Jesus your tongue gets as big as a cabbage with the trenchmouth and the pyovitis or whatever pyo something they call it and blessed Christ knows what else terrible tetniss germs thriving and jumping about in the very spit of a person's mouth

there's a boy over on 69th Street whose father works his fingers to the bone in the fish store for those three Italian brothers who swallowed no more water than it would take to put in your eye and his teeth fell out of his gums they went all rotten one at a time all black and full of pus they were and the poor man and his wife a tarty-looking woman God bless the mark spend all their time at this Novena and that Novena but by Jesus Christ Almighty teeth can't grow back even if you pray until your knees fall off your legs with cancer

the best altar boy at St. Anselm's had both of his ears explode into flinders it's the God's truth and out came animals yes little animals the likes of which nobody ever saw

Mary Pickford almost died from just a drop of polluted water at some fancy Florida beach going up her nose it was her fortune and the smart jew doctors the stars have that saved her

the Pope himself they begged him to come on their knees and bless the ocean and purify it where a bunch of ignorant hunkies killed a goat or some dumb animal right on the beach and they call themselves Catholics

that clean-cut boy who went to St. Francis Xavier and was engaged to be married to a girl whose father is a sergeant of detectives fell over dead one evening over a glass of beer and it was no accident that he'd been at Coney Island all day with his brother a fine boy who is now just this side of a blithering idiot

scientists in the paper say that every disease known to the world and God bless us and save us not known at all is to be found in the ocean right there it's the filthiest beach in the world

and the worst thing is that sometimes the germs will be in somebody who thinks he's smart and knows it all for years and years and all of a sudden when he's twenty or thirty years old he'll go blind or deaf or crippled or his nose will start to rot off so the doctors say they call it a dormon disease

That night, Red lies awake for a long time, willing the water he took into his mouth, the water he swallowed, harmless. He employs charms and formulas in strict order, e.g.,

Nothing Scoville's.

Nothing Scoville's.

Nothing Scoville's Scoville's Nothing.

Scoville's Nothing.

Scoville's Nothing.

Mother always says that Scoville's is clean and the people very decent, regular people. He falls asleep and dreams of Nancy O'Neill. She has her bathing suit on and her arms are crossed tightly over her chest but she is also stark naked. She is only naked from the waist down. Red keeps trying to see between her legs but he can't. Her arms are crossed tightly over her chest and she asks him if he likes to feel her twat. He wakes up, his nose is stuffed, mouth bone dry. Dry from the salt water and pollution. His penis is erect and stiff and swollen, a sure sign of the disease of which he is quickly dying.

SEVENTEEN

❖

Grandma and Mother are having a conversation, but Mother is not doing much talking. Her side of the colloquy manifests itself mostly in sobs. Red, groggy with a fever from the mumps, lies on the couch in the front room, sliding pleasantly in and out of the clarity of apprehension. But he hears that something, or everything, is Mother's fault, she has broken or damaged her life, his life, Father's life, and goodhearted Grandma and Grandpa.

Grandma says that she's fed up with finger smudges on the glasses and dishes and Mother couldn't even hold the good job she had in the bank when she was single, she doesn't appreciate the roof over her head. Red, well, Red is thoroughly disobedient, a devil of a boy, Mother can't hold a job even now, does she remember the spectacle she made of herself as a waitress? Grandpa almost dies of shame with the dirty-grey shirts Mother said she washes, *washes*? And Mother still can't iron a handkerchief worth a fart in a gale of wind, they're all wrinkles and creases like everything she puts her hand to, it's all Grandma's fault for she was too goodhearted and spoiled her rotten, may God forgive her, when she was a little girl, oh

Jesus, when Grandma thinks of her little yellow dresses and her blue dresses, beautiful, starched linen with dozens of cunning little pleats and her little socks and hair ribbon to match, she always looked as if she just stepped out of a bandbox. It was those real American-girl looks that caught the eye of that nice refined boy who worked for Dun & Bradstreet, Red is Mother's responsibility, sure, but Mother knows of the sacrifices, two more mouths to feed, not to speak of the electric bill and the gas, the soap, Red eats like a horse, the desserts that cost a king's ransom! Mother could well have put up with and tried to understand Father's little failings, he's only flesh and blood, he takes a drink too many now and then, what real man doesn't? To have the poor man mortified by Mother's carryings-on with that mollycoddle of a whatever he was, some kind of a store clerk or a sissy of a schoolteacher while Father was out drinking himself into a stupor with his broken heart and who can blame the man? God knows, the work in the bank wasn't too hard, a nice clean job with decent people in and out all day to break the monotony, Mother was waited on hand and foot, Grandpa wouldn't let her lift a finger, more fool he, although Grandma doted on her as well. She was much too good for Father, all right, yes, when all is said and done, he has a lot of the bogtrotter in him, but Mother surely neglected Red while Father was out looking for work to pay the mortgage on that little pitiful crackerbox of a house in Flatbush, and she'll have to answer to her Maker for that. That was a hard-luck house if Grandma ever saw one, the first time she stepped inside it she knew that they wouldn't have a single day of happiness there and she was right, she knows that she and Grandpa were not welcome there, with the cold sandwiches and a little picayune salad and maybe a glass or two of beer, and the little of *that* begrudged them, and it was all that Father could do to drive them back home in the new car that they soon repossessed on him. What kind of man was that clerk, some kind of Englishman or an English jew, all the English are jews way down deep, even the king and queen, beJesus they're always marrying each other, their cousins and nieces and uncles and even their sisters if the truth be known, what kind of a man takes advantage of a young wife with a child not yet three years old? It's a mortal sin! What heartbreak Mother brought Grandma and Grandpa when that black day came as Grandma knew it would, Father so drunk that he was clawing at his face and climbing the walls, God help us, and telling Grandpa man to man that Mother was no more than that little fart's tramp, butter wouldn't melt in his mouth he said, oh the poor man was crying out to God to help him and with the puke all over his overcoat. The modest dresses Mother once wore, to the bank, the job she lost, and Red is ungrateful and sassing Grandma every day of the week, and the silk stockings with Mother's skirts none too long, poor Father, the ignorant lout of a paddy, he was made to think he had to improve himself beyond his station or ability, he lost what little mind he has almost, it was a sad day when Mother and Father and Red moved from the neighborhood into that little shack of a house so far away, no one could get there by subway or even a God damned trolley, except with transfers and more transfers and standing in the bitter cold on some strange corner in a neighborhood full of foreigners, just to pay a visit and get, *maybe*, a ham sandwich and a cup of tea. Silk stockings and blouses that would make a floozie blush, oh yes, Grandma knew that something was going on with that little strutting salesman or pencil pusher, with his pomaded hair and his little moustache and his scented handkerchief, a patch on a man's ass he was, and Grandpa tried to say something to make Mother come to her senses, there's always some dried egg on his egg cup lately. Maybe Mother and Red would like to find out what it's like to be out on the street, or maybe living with Katy in Jersey, with her crippled idiot of a bus-driver husband sitting drooling all day, and her son, Francis, who thinks he's God's gift to bookkeepers, too God damned good to eat a boiled potato nowadays, la de da, and where did the lipstick on the teacup come from last night? Mother ought to be ashamed of herself, well, she was *never* much of a house-keeper, she'll confess to that herself, always with her nose stuck in a movie magazine or a novel from the drugstore, in her housedress till all hours of the afternoon. She still doesn't try to look like the mother of a twelve-year-old gawm of a boy should, with her high heels and her little hats just to go out and buy a dime's worth of hard rolls, it's no wonder that Red's Father was suspicious, what's sauce for the goose. That's what Grandma always says. It wouldn't hurt a bit for Mother and Red to go and see what life is like with a down-at-the-heels streel like Katy or maybe Jimmy Kenny will take Mother and her disobedient hoodlum of a son in, God knows that Mother has plenty to jaw about with the bleached peroxide blonde hooer of a polack cashier, Marie or Mary or Margie that he has the nerve to call his wife, and his poor old hag of a mother, a saint on earth, crawling up to the altar rail at six o'clock Mass every morning of her life, a lot of good it's done her, Mother, oh yes indeed, Mother understands Marie or Mary or Margie and Grandma knows why, with her disgracing Father, *and* he said, the poor simpleton with the horns sticking out of his head, in his *own house*, it's hard to blame the man for becoming a drunken ruined bum, although to be fair he always had a weakness for the booze, a failing that Mother, a well-brought-up girl with a good business background and a high-school commercial diploma could have put her foot down about if she'd had any gumption. No wonder, no wonder at all that Red is in the way of becoming a moron, locking himself in the bathroom for hours, and staring at the ads in the Sunday papers for corsets and drawers, he's surely well on the path to being a homomorphodite by the age of fifteen. The potatoes are burned too often, Red is in the class with the criminal dagos and Armenian fruit peddlers with their fingernails black as the ace of spades, every one of them crawling with cooties, can't speak a word of English, God knows what the city is coming to, it was a paradise when Grandma was a girl. Grandma hears things, oh yes indeed, don't worry about that, even though Mother and Grandpa try to keep her in the dark, they're both as happy as clams that she doesn't go out and make a display of herself every day, but she hears things, she has her ways. Yes, Mother and Grandpa, the two of them have always made her feel like a stranger in her own house, they wouldn't shed a tear were she to be struck deaf, dumb, and blind, or *dead*, for that matter. She may as well be dead already with the disgrace and heartbreak of a divorced daughter who acts like a floozie and a grandson on the road to being a shiftless bum like his Father. There's no excuse whatsoever for the spinach to be sandy, Mother, by the living Christ, has all day to clean the house and Grandma will *not* have the radio on for hours and hours in the afternoon with the soap operas, a waste of electricity, who ever heard of such foolishness? No wonder that greaseball gorilla of a bookmaker on the corner tips his hat to Mother, the perfect gentleman, and she skipping along in silk stockings to show off her legs, and her high heels, in the pouring torrents of rain, there's not an ounce of shame in the woman. When they're all runs we'll see if the big pyzon says hello then, a thirty-year-old woman acting like a little chippie. What *did* happen to Mr. After-Shave Cologne, that pomaded little cock of the walk of a tie salesman, blessed Jesus? What happened? Grandma knows damn well what happened. He went scurrying back to his potwalloper drudge of a wife the minute Father walked out and there he was, Mr. Floorwalker, faced with the abandoned wife and her four-year-old child, the pissabed! The black eyes that Mother got from Father, they broke Grandma's heart, but God knows that they were justified, and Mother can bet her bottom dollar that they gave that little sissy midget a push out the door in the right direction, Jesus Christ and all His Saints in Heaven will never know what attracted Mother to such a little runt, but she's had plenty of time to rue the day he came along, with his suits all the fashion. And if there's one more ironing scorch on a shirt or so much as a handkerchief, Grandma will take the expense out of Red's suppers, and that's the truth, as God is her judge. Let his ne'er-do-well Father buy him his supper, and his breakfast and lunch too, God save the poor man, he's had his cross to bear. With Mother, sad to say.

And a bum dronker cruss trampel sup, a chup pie, unc cockawk, a morpho morphite mordite doron. Sob, sob, sob. Red sleeps.

EIGHTEEN

❖

Red is a connoisseur of odds and ends, and knows that things which seem inexplicable will often be illuminated, if not understood, in due time; that solid, intractable, irrefutable facts are almost always, and without fail, interchangeable with other solid, intractable, irrefutable facts; and that nothing, no matter how clear or obvious or settled, can be taken for granted. Above all, he is convinced that wholly discrete phenomena or elements of information, placed side by side, ultimately explain each other.

Some of the things in the cellar storage bin don't belong to Grandma or to Grandpa or to Mother or to Father but to an "Alice Magrino," a name often brought up when Father is being excoriated.

One of the old, creased photographs in the cellar storage bin is of what seems to be either a dead, bloated cow or a large, shapeless sack of what may be flour. On the back of the photograph is the name, ALICE, and the date, 1921.

Mouse turds dissolve completely in chicken soup, vegetable soup, green split-pea soup, and bean soup.

The cunning knife-sharp pleats on the yellow dresses, blue

dresses, white dresses, and pink dresses that Mother wore as a
little girl were laboriously ironed by the orphaned cousin Katy,
whose failure to do so perfectly was the invariable occasion for
her to be beaten black and blue, by Grandma, with a wooden
yardstick.

A "Theresa McKenna" has something to do with Grandpa's
life as a young man. She is occasionally brought up in conversation, wherein she is variously described, by Grandma, as
crosseyed, walleyed, knock-kneed, box-ankled, stringy-haired,
pimply-faced, lard-assed, potbellied, louse-ridden, sanctimo-
nious, hypocritical, stuck-up, common, needle-nosed, bald,
squinty, overdressed, shameless, trashy, and man-crazy.

Mother sometimes secretly drinks from Grandpa's bottle of
Wilson's "That's All" whiskey.

Whenever Grandma mentions Grandpa's mandolin,
Grandpa smiles the same smile that Uncle John had on his face
in his casket.

Grandma flirts with Mr. Svensen when he comes to collect
the rent, then later bawls Grandpa out for giving him too large
a hooker of whiskey.

A few drops of urine are undetectable in the glass of water
in which Grandma keeps her teeth.

If Red looks glum when Mother is buying something in
Bloom's Drugs, Mr. Bloom gives him three Hershey's Kisses
instead of two, and it serves the kike chump right.

Red gives Grandpa two packs of Lucky Strikes for his birthday, and Grandpa, mysteriously, hugs him.

When Mother goes to the Novena on Tuesday nights she
comes home smelling like Sen-Sen or peppermint.

Red sees Mother naked one day and is upset to discover
that she has what seems to be fur between her legs, like hooers.

Red immediately goes out of the neighborhood to break the

one-dollar bill that the old man in the park gave him to let him play with his thing a little.

When Red pretends deafness and lets his mouth hang open and his eyes glaze over, Grandma's purple-faced rage is worth the beating that she invariably gives him. After these beatings, Red often turns his attention to her false teeth.

When Red begins the Lord's Prayer, "Our Father, Who farts in heaven, how low be Thy name," and the nuns hear him but can't *hear* him, the world of guile opens up for him in all its devious splendor.

To answer Grandma's rhetorical questions infuriates her; to ignore those questions to which she wants answers infuriates her.

One evening, after supper, when Mother is preparing to go to the movies on dish night—Grandma's treat, for which Mother will pay and pay and pay—Red is bewildered yet somehow thrilled to see her slip a green glass saucer into her handbag.

Father drunkenly introduces Red to a drunken young woman with an enormous bust and spindly legs, whom he calls Alice, his kid sister. Or cousin. A friend of his. A niece.

Red's essential understanding of life is rooted in the belief that there are few situations that cannot be improved upon, rescued by, or utterly destroyed by a blank disingenuousness.

Red knows that people have to live until they have to die, and this fills him with a meager joy, for it means that *all* of them will die. That all of them *have* to die.

NINETEEN

❖

Grandma often wants to hurt Red for reasons that remain her secret. At such times, she patiently constructs an edifice of Red's wrongdoing that, when complete, stands as witness to his crimes, crimes that must be punished. Sometimes these aberrant exercises in domestic sadism take Red into areas of his mind that are darkly inexplicable, but that, even so, act as antidotes to the poisons that surround and invade him. Not that these poisons are not then interiorized: they are, indeed, interiorized, and transformed. The world lurches forward, its terrors unabated.

One day, Grandma says that she thinks that Red has been playing with her false teeth where they rest, as usual, in a chipped glass half-full of water. She says that the glass has been moved a little. She knows that *she* didn't move it! She says that Red has a bad habit of sticking his snotty nose where it doesn't belong. However, Grandma laughs, and laughs again, her sagging breasts shaking inside her torn housedress; Red *cannot* have been *playing* with her *teeth* because he knows that she would beat him raw if he ever dared. There's something, though, Grandma says, about her glass. It's not in the right place. Oh it's in the right place, but it's not in the *right* place. Red says, with the semi-idiotic candor he has almost perfected, that he would never *ever* play with Grandma's teeth, or with anything of Grandma's. He arranges such a look of awestruck incredulity on his face that Grandma is actually silenced for a moment.

Red, who earlier plunged a feces-covered forefinger into Grandma's glass, knows that his ordure did not visibly affect the water, and he knows that he did not move, nor did he even touch the glass. He intensifies his idiotic look, catching his lower lip with his greenish buck teeth. He is, narrowly speaking, right: he did not move the glass, he is innocent.

Mother says, from the kitchen, where she is scrubbing the oven, that there's no reason, really no reason for Red to. Why would Red. She says that Red has no reason to. She says why Grandma's teeth.

Grandma says that Red is to get that look of a mongolian idiot off his face before she *slaps* it off his face. She steps forward and slaps Red so hard that tears instantly pop into his eyes. He tries out a shy smile. Grandma bangs him sharply in the mouth with the back of her left hand, so that her wedding ring draws blood from his lower lip. She says that he's a grinning monkey and that God will strike him dead some day for making a mockery of poor stupid morons, God bless the mark.

Mother stops scrubbing the oven. She says that Grandma *heard* Red say. She heard Red tell her. And why would Red. Grandma says that Mother can go and tell her sad tale to the cheap, common waitress in the Surprise that she's made a friend of, Jesus Christ on the Cross knows why, and leave the black-hearted mongrel of a boy to her. Grandma looks into Red's face, decides against its current expression of pain, and hits him a crisp blow on his cut lip. Red turns away, holding his mouth, and Grandma, who is freshly sweating into the stale sweat of her clothes, says that if Red ever ever ever even goes *near* her teeth, she'll cut the legs out from under him. She'll beat him to within an inch of his life. She'll make him wish he lived with the polacks and wops and shanty paddies in the Catholic orphanage where he'll see how the nuns treat him when he gives them his back talk, not, to be sure, like here, where he's coddled and babied and spoiled rotten. She emphasizes these last two words with two brisk slashes of a leather belt across Red's bare legs. Spoiled! Rotten! Grandma says again, adding a pair of welts to the first two. Then she begins to whale away at him at will, her determination an almost holy thing.

Mother comes all the way out of the kitchen and actually raises her voice in protest at the frenzied assault on Red. His legs are swollen and bright pink with crimson welts crisscrossing his calves, his lip is bleeding, and he cowers, half-bent over, in the corner. Grandma screams at Mother that this is the thanks she gets for buying her a brand-new pair of pumps from Enna Jettick so that she'll not disgrace herself and Grandma too looking like the charity case she really *is* when she walks the streets, and as for Red, he doesn't care that if it were not for Grandma—and Grandpa, the poor goodhearted slob is working himself into his grave—he'd surely be wearing cast-off rags alive with fleas in an orphanage run by mean, hatchet-faced nuns with the cold hearts of Methodist Protestants whose lives are so rotten that they can't rest until everybody else's life is rotten too. Only God in His mercy can love them with their rosaries that they beat the helpless orphans with, and their creeping Jesus and their bless me this and bless me that, they're a curse on the Church, may God forgive her. Mother screams louder for Grandma to stop! To STOP! She says that she doesn't care shite about nuns or orphans or their rags, she says to *stop!*

Grandma stops whipping Red and stands, panting and

sweaty, her shrunken lips spasmodically working over her gums. Red cringes in the corner by the radio, in a half-crouch against the wall, rubbing his hot, stinging legs. He says in a voice so low that he can hardly hear himself, the word *cunt*. He has no truly clear idea of what the word means, but he knows that it is really dirty, worse than *shit*. It is, he knows, absolutely forbidden, and its dangerous opacity seems the perfect descriptive for Grandma.

Grandma looks over at Red and asks him what he just said, what was that he said, what word did he say. Red says that he said *crumb*, and then, in a remarkably calm panic, he picks up from the floor a dust ball, shows it, fleetingly, to Grandma, and then eats it. He says that it's a cracker crumb, so that's why he said *crumb*, as he chews dramatically, then swallows. Grandma steps toward him, raises her hand, and says that he's not to eat dusty trash from the floor, what kind of a pig is he, she's sick and tired of Red having to see Dr. Drescher, the doddering old quack from the year one, who is rich enough already.

Red glances at Grandma and thinks *dust ball*, she is a *dust ball*. If she's a *cunt* and a *cunt* is a *crumb* and a *crumb* is a *dust ball*, she's a *dust ball*. The other way: a *dust ball* is a *crumb* is a *cunt*. What a wonderful sound, dull and thick, a Grandma word, *cunt*.

Red sees her then as Grandma Cunt, especially at this very moment, when he and Grandma and Mother realize, at the same time, that he has, in his pain and fright, wet his pants and his legs and his socks and shoes and the rug.

The rug! Oh God.

Grandma Cunt's mouth closes into a thin, malicious smile, and Red looks down at his sopping wet shorts clinging to his crotch and thighs. His burning legs are soothed by the urine that washes them.

Next time, shit *and* piss will go into the teeth glass, and maybe he'll stick his thing in too.

He begins to shiver and sob in his humiliation and embarrassment. Mother embraces him as Grandma goggles at them both. She shakes her head at this further rent in domestic stability.

TWENTY

❖

Red shells the peas without having to be told. He pulls three-day-old copies of *The Sun* and the *Journal-American* off the dumbwaiter to save Grandpa the trouble. He cleans his plate, drinks his tea without slurping or spilling it, brings Grandpa his shoeshine box. He tempers his violent, raucous, inappropriate laughter, cries just enough, but not too much, when Grandma wallops him, says thank God and pardon me before leaving the table. He scrubs his knuckles and cleans the black dirt out from under his fingernails. He wears the clip-on red-and-yellow polka-dot bow tie that Mr. Svensen gave him for his birthday, brushes his shoes, pulls down the hated ear flaps on his woollen cap before going out to play, oils his roller skates. He accepts second helpings of slimy rhubarb and eats it with notable relish. He looks somber and agonized when Grandma tells him, yet again, of how Mother almost died giving birth to him, a bad boy even then. He combs the tangles out of his mat of hair and even gives himself a part, of sorts. He steals fewer of Grandpa's Lucky Strikes. He claps his hands with almost convincing delight when Grandma tells him that he may help Mother color Easter eggs again, and tops the astonishing display off by shouting oh boy! and wow! He stops carelessly pissing all over the toilet seat and the bathroom floor. He battles his recurrent vision of Grandma falling out one window or another. He volunteers to beat the rugs up on the roof. He goes from D to C in both Effort and Conduct on his report card.

What a boy! What a fine boy!

He cures the sick, the lame, the infected, and the insane, raises the dead, revolutionizes the teaching of geography, distills whiskey, rolls perfect cigarettes, squares the circle, wins both Golden Gloves and Silver Skates championships and shakes hands with the Mayor, clears up his and everybody else's pimples, makes clothes for the entire apartment building, halts Father's drunkenness, marries Mother off to an ex-priest who has discovered the cure for cancer, pyovitis, consumption, galloping pneumonia, malaise, general depression, morphoditism, and bad breath, goes to Brooklyn Tech and rethinks the bases of differential calculus, finds a million dollars in an ash can and gives it to the Sisters of Charity, beats Fredo in boxing, wrestling, running, jumping, knuckles, twenty-one, arm wrestling, Indian wrestling, and the decathlon, learns to drive, learns to fly, learns to cook, sew, knit and crochet, learns to perform small yet necessary plumbing repairs, turns the front room into a compact yet fully equipped gym, tries on Mother's clothes and decides, whenever he feels like it, to be a girl, gives a speech in the school auditorium on Father's honest life as a porter, cleaning man, fill-in bartender, and washer of taxis, confesses in somewhat hazy detail his imperfectly impure thoughts of Isabelle Stiles, Rhoda Roy, Virginia Christie, Annette Euphemia, Mrs. Meltzer, Dolores Scupari, Helen Walsh, Claire Alessio, and Dixie Dugan, does penance, receives the Eucharist in a blinding golden light amid the sound of a choir, and then gives each of these lovely young girls, as well as Mrs. Meltzer, but excluding the not quite real Dixie Dugan, one perfect hybrid yellow rose, anonymously, stops abusing himself, for his now perfectly tuned religious perception allows him a glimpse of Hell, which seems to be solely populated by billions of self-polluting boys surrounded by delighted devils, paints the kitchen, lays new linoleum, buys summer window awnings in the heraldic family colors, and gives Grandma a priceless antique diamond tiara in appreciation of the fact that God has persuaded her to put her teeth in for meals and wear underclothes.

What a wonderful boy! What a wonderful boy!

Grandma says that Red's acts, his wonderful and thoughtful acts, are pitiable and laughable, because it is as plain as the nose on your face that Red is doing all these things, these namby-pamby Bible-thumping things, butter wouldn't melt in his mouth things, to pull the wool over Grandma's eyes, fat chance, ha *ha*!

It's a wise child that can fool a grandmother.

She tells him that there will be no more movies on Saturdays, the serials are rotting the brains out of his skull, the few that he has, poor lamebrain, and she does not want him watching those sissy boys they call actors nowadays like Tom Wayne or whatever his name is, and that every penny that he earns carrying groceries on Saturday mornings for those nigger-rich women putting on airs so that they can't carry a bag of day-old bread and wilted vegetables and a soup bone, too good to carry a bag of leavings a block or two, *every penny* is to be turned over to Grandma to help meet the expenses of the house, it's time for Red to give something rather than take, take, take, God in His paradise knows that Mother can't get a job or hold on to one if by chance a miracle happens and somebody makes a mistake and hires her. That will be a cold day in Hell.

There will be no penny for candy on the way back to school or after school, it's a waste of good money and it rots the teeth out of his head, and God knows that Red's teeth look like the green proud harp flag of free Ireland as it is, by Jesus.

He can forget about long pants this year, clothes cost a king's ransom, Depression or no Depression, he can wear his knickers with a patch here and there, until he's thirteen years old and maybe even longer than that if he can't keep a civil tongue in his bullet head. A boy who wears long pants has to be a *man* and Red is but a baby with his complaining, and he still wets the bed once in a while, it's disgusting.

And Grandma says that she'll not accept, if her life depended on it, his *diamond* tiara, which *diamonds* look a lot like glass, for though his heart may be in the right place and the kind thought somewhat of a shock to her, she'll be damned if she'll put in her teeth day in and day out, they're a trial and a torment, it serves her right that she went to some American quack of a dentist, and as for underwear, it's only a degenerative morphodite like Red who would notice such a thing, looking at his own Grandma like that, by Christ it's not natural, Red should hang his head in shame, is that what these old-maid nuns teach him, and Grandma punches him in the ear to make certain that her considered opinions register clearly with him.

Spare the rod and spoil the fine, wonderful, thoughtful boy.

TWENTY ONE

❖

Red has tasks and chores, jobs, duties, and responsibilities, desires, and fantasies; as well as obligations and habits, some salutary, others profane. They are, variously, diurnal, nocturnal, weekly, bi-weekly, monthly, bi-monthly, semi-annual, and annual. Although neither Red nor anyone else knows it, some are, more or less, in place for life, while others may be considered manifestations of a fragmented childhood, to disappear in time. Ah, in time.

What are these tasks, etc.? May some represent all, or, perhaps more precisely, may some be proffered as samples of all?

To make forays into the sinister dark; bear paper bags heavy with groceries; maim and kill vermin large and small; set mouse traps; smear J-O paste on slices of potato; receive insults; shine shoes; endure humiliations; wash his feet; smash cockroaches; empty ashtrays; run errands; take Scott's Emulsion, Fletcher's Castoria, and Phillips' Milk of Magnesia; absorb blows of varied strength and accuracy; suffer contumely; stare at pages of incomprehensible grammar lessons; put up with torturous cavities; fear Grandma's corset; leave the bathroom door ajar; unplug all the lamps in thunderstorms; recite, cheeks aflame, Grandma's instructions as to her strict

requirements to Phil the kike butcher, Mr. Dreyer the nazi grocer, Dom the thieving greengrocer, and whatshisname, the
guinea fish peddler; clean splattered urine from the toilet and
the bathroom floor; act like a degenerate; tremblingly hide and
then tremblingly return to their place Grandma's thin leather
belts; abuse himself though Hell looms, the Virgin Mary
weeps, Jesus feels the cruel nails in His flesh once again, and
the chains of Satan relentlessly clank in the courtyard; ignore
snubs subtle and overt; perfect and fine-tune his idiot look; be
incomprehensibly excited by Mother's high heels; throw away
the pink-and-violet plaid muffler given him by his cousin
Theresa; sniff Grandma's crepe de chine dresses; rescue girls in
their underpants from Yellow Fiends who have them strapped
onto tables; look for lice in his hair and the seams of his
clothes; beg for and be denied a Little Orphan Annie Ovaltine
shaker, a Tom Mix Checkerboard Square telescope, and an
Official Lone Ranger Badge plus an Authentic Something;
rummage through Grandma's handbags searching for money;
carry the wet wash up to the roof; kill Sal Rongo and his
brother, Vinnie, with an Invisible Death Ray; press his leg
lightly against Mrs. Meltzer's leg as she shows him how to add
fractions; puzzle over the legend on a paper napkin from
Fritz's Tavern Steaks and Chops, "Handlome Il Al Handlome
Doel"; scheme to discover ways to look up Helen Cordell's
skirt; steal pennies from Feinie's newsstand when his half-blind
brother minds the store; do battle with the slavering monsters
who want to cut off Mother's arrestingly blond hair and kill
the water rats who wish to suck on it; pretend not to care
when Mrs. Long stands him in the corner for being a block-
head; pretend not to care when Sister Rose of Lima beats his
palms with a ruler for being a sinful dumbbell; endure
reproach; fly in his red bi-plane over the Burning Sands of the
Sahara and the Steaming Jungles of the Congo to rescue girls

in their underpants; try to draw like Chester Gould; force raucous laughter while watching animated cartoons; inspect the
neighbors' discarded newspapers on the dumbwaiter for stains
and unmentionable matter; tunnel into the Molten Center of
the Earth with Madeleine Carroll as companion; lasso, wrango,
and something-something li'l' dogies; save the nuns in Spain
from being made to show their heads in public by the dirty
Communists; win a game of king's or boxball; eat a T-bone
porterhouse sirloin; be Wimpy; borrow Cheech's eight-page
bible, "Blondie"; buy all the new comic books; watch his
cousin Theresa piss in Warren's cellar; lie about everything in
the confessional, regularly, sinfully, fearfully, yet without
remorse; listen to and spread filthy stories about Father Gra-
ham and Mother Superior; claim to be Protestant to try and get
out of going to religious instruction; smoke a pipe; take sips of
Grandpa's whiskey; in a trance, push Grandma in front of a
trolley; get a Buck Rogers Disintegrator; shell peas, soak beans,
rinse spinach, wash lettuce, peel potatoes, pit peaches, squeeze
lemons, section grapefruit, dry dishes; laboriously try to read,
unsuccessfully, a Tom Swift book, a Hardy Boys book, a Boy
Ranchers book, and a Dave Dawson book; burn Big Mickey at
the stake; learn the words to "Make Believe Ballroom"; go to
and never ever return from Festive Méjico!

TWENTY TWO

❖

Grandma rarely answers the sudden doorbell and forbids any-one else to answer it. Unless the ring is expected, the door stays firmly shut, and the family waits in total silence until the poten-tial intruder leaves. Grandma says that it could be *anybody* and the hell with them! She is always indignant toward the unknown visitor on the other side of the door. *Anybody*. Few visitors are ever expected, and Grandma has no understanding of hospital-ity. A surprise ring at the door doubtlessly announces, according to Grandma, a distant relative of Grandpa's looking for a hand-out, a distant relative of Grandma's with a hard-luck story, some hooligan ne'er-do-well working his way through college, a reli-gious maniac waving around a fat Protestant bible all colored ribbons, a lazy bohunk or nigger with a filthy rag pretending to want to wash the windows, a fat drunken cop selling lottery tickets to help the rest of his shanty pals, a fat drunken fireman selling lottery tickets for the benefit of the forty thieves in his engine house, the local Democrat ward-heeler looking for votes with the veins in his nose by Christ as blue as the sky, or maybe Clark Gable himself selling gold bricks, a picture that makes Grandma laugh coldly, but laugh nonetheless.

On this particular day, the first of the month, the ring, which comes at five in the afternoon, is indeed expected, for this is rent day, and Mr. Svensen invariably arrives at this hour with his ja-this and ja-that to collect the rent and suck up to Grandpa, the awful pushover of a man, for a couple of whiskeys. Grandma says she'd like to "ja-ja" *him*, the old fart. Yet at the ring she pinches her cheeks to bring up their color.

It is not, however, Mr. Svensen, but a thin, closely shaven, pale young priest, his dusty black suit, greenish with age, a startling contrast to his immaculate white collar. He crosses the threshold and Grandpa steps back, not in invitation but surprise. Grandma calls down the hallway for Grandpa to close the door so that the neighbors won't have such a grand time of it finding out *all* their business. Her command falters and trails off as she sees the priest: he is actually in the apartment! Grandpa closes the door behind him and, somewhat genially, directs him down the hallway toward the dining room and the stunned figure of Grandma, immobile in her usual tatters and rags. Grandpa says that the priest is collecting for the Missions, for the priests and nuns and brothers doing God's work in the black jungles of Africa. The priest stands still and smiles tentatively at Grandma, who is staring, agog, over her glasses at his pasty, scraped face and the ripe pimple on the wing of his nose.

Grandma fears priests, and never goes to Mass. There is something far away about them, and they have an inhuman smell that suggests strange doings. They are magicians. That Jesus Christ arrives, in His actual tortured Being, upon the altar, terrifies Grandma. That she is expected to eat His actual Body, drink His actual Blood, shakes her, and the taste of the Eucharistic wafer nauseates her. The last time Grandma received, years and years ago, she threw the wafer up on the floor in her pew and waited for God to destroy her with a bolt of fire. In her abject whimpering agony of fear, she wet herself. She is certain that the celebrant priest knew of her blasphemous shame.

The young priest is constructing, haltingly, his case for charity. Grandpa, bewildered in his strange role as host, looks toward the kitchen where the whiskey is. Grandma adjusts her hairnet, closes her near-toothless mouth, pulls the neck of her housedress closed, yanks down her ragged skirt, attempts to hide her wisps of stockings by placing one leg in front of the other, and finally shuffles in her broken slippers to the bedroom to get her purse, to give the interloper money, to send him and his magic out the door.

Red watches the bizarre choreography of this scene, and suddenly into the shadows of his ignorance comes a steady hellfire light, and he is, for a flash, Grandma, he is inside Grandma's mind, righteous, cruel, mean, and wonderfully, beautifully, wholly terror-stricken! *Red comprehends*. He steps humbly toward the priest, who stands between the diningroom table and the broken Morris chair, and takes a position next to Grandpa: Grandpa's ally, Grandpa's assistant, Grandpa's eager, devout, and loving grandson. He looks at this pantywaist sissy of a priest, this pallid creeping Jesus, as Grandma says, this patch on a real man's ass, yet, God save us all, ten times better than a moneygrubbing Protestant with their God damned parades and their ice-cream!

Out of the corner of his eye, Red sees Grandma, pale and sweaty, her purse open and in one hand—a *dollar bill*. Her eyes are wide with anxiety and she watches the priest with disguised alarm. At any moment, he might, he might, at any moment he's liable to send her to her Maker, unconfessed, oh God keep us! Red looks directly at the priest, bitter contempt for this dope and for Grandma settling upon him.

Then Red begins to ask the priest detailed questions about

the Missions, his face taking on a sweet and sickening mask of piety and reverent curiosity. An answer leads to another question and to an elaboration of the original question, then to a hesitant and utterly stupid opinion about the faith that the priest nervously corrects. The priest shifts from foot to foot and finally sits on a straight chair! Grandma looks at Red with venomous loathing in her eyes, her thin mouth clamped in a fierce concrete grin. Grandpa asks the priest if he would like a glass of water or, maybe, ah, uh, a sup of whiskey to keep out the cold? Red smiles benignly.

Oh how wonderful to be a Catholic! Oh how interesting to hear about the ignorant nigger savages and the one true Church! Red abandonedly asks Grandma if *she* doesn't think it's all swell as Grandpa hands the priest a half-tumbler of whiskey and holds his own glass up in a jovial salute. Red smiles again, thinking up another question, maybe one about mortal sin. Or the Joyful Mysteries.

To the Church's health! To the Missions! To Grandma's terror! May it grow and prosper!

Here's luck!

Red does not look again at Grandma, whose face reveals that she knows, of course, of course, she knows.

TWENTY THREE

❖

On the morning of New Year's Day, Grandpa sets out on the credenza the two dozen ladyfingers brought home from Ebinger's. He has carefully arranged them on a rectangular plate of fine China, used but once or twice a year. Next to it he places a bottle of The Christian Brothers pale-dry sherry and four delicate crystal glasses. He steps back and looks at this display and says that it's not New Year's without ladyfingers and sherry, a comment that causes Grandma to sneer that there's no fool like an old fool. She says that this is the last year or may God strike her dead that she'll let Grandpa throw good money away on his Church of Ireland airs and notions. You'd think he was never converted to the true faith. Mother seems slightly happy. Red, although he knows better, looks at the dainty refreshments and considers that something nice might happen today. He knows better.

Grandpa, freshly shaved and smelling of witch hazel, a dark tie luminous against his crisply starched white shirt, puts on his suitcoat, muffler, and overcoat, and picks up his homburg. He says that his New Year's visits won't take long, he's only going to pay his respects to his sisters and Aunt Maddy and he'll be back before one, in plenty of time for dinner, and to say hello to well-wishers and have a glass of wine with them! The rest of the family looks silently at this figure of astounding self-delusion. Fantastic. He knows better. Grandpa leaves.

New Year's Day truly begins with Grandma telling Mother how to get the ham ready, how to get the string beans or peas or spinach ready, how to do this and that and that and this, how to do everything. For Mother can do nothing, nothing, nothing at all but drive away husbands and spoil children. Red goes into the bathroom and peacefully abuses himself.

The smell of dinner cooking, New Year's Day continues. Is it Brussels sweet potatoes sprouts whose aroma fills the house? Dessert will be Jell-O, green Jell-O with chunks of Dole pineapple caught in its glutinous translucency. Outside, the air is crystal clear and the remnants of a recent snowfall are turned solid ice. Red looks out the window past the roofs to the Kings County Lighting Company's gas tanks huge and squat on the horizon and wonders if they will ever blow up. Gone, everything gone in a flash. He glances at the ladyfingers and the sherry. Soon Grandpa will be home. Soon dinner will be eaten. Finished. And soon after?

And soon after the apartment will be festive with neighbors, friends, and relatives in constant, joyful flux! Grandpa will have to buy more ladyfingers and sherry! Grandma will grumble goodheartedly like those fucking old ladies in the movies with hearts of gold!

Mother changes into her good black dress with the faint gold stripes, puts on make-up and high heels. She looks beautiful, and Red goes over and puts his arms around her, feels her warm flesh through the dress, smells her perfume flowery and remote. Grandma asks her who the hell she thinks she's going to impress all dolled up like a five hundred dollar millionaire. Like Paddy's pig. Like Astor's pet horse. Like a nigger on

Christmas. She surveys the table setting and farts, then tells Mother that the water glasses should be here or should be there or should be somewhere something. Red feels sick for a second. Grandpa comes in.

They are not halfway through the meal, eaten in sullen silence broken only by Grandma's comments on how salty the ham didn't Mother something, how soggy the beans didn't she tell Mother to, how dried out the sweet potatoes didn't she warn Mother of, when Grandma shifts her attention from the meal that is not fit for the pigs really, probably because Mother was so het up about putting on that dress with the low neck that makes her look like a slut not to mention its short skirt and the high heels and the bright-red lipstick, shameful, she shifts her attention abruptly to ask Grandpa about his skinflint sisters and if Aunt Maddy still suffers from the scrofula, God bless the mark, and does the old biddy still sit in the dark with only a kerosene lamp from when Napoleon was a cadet to save a penny on the light bill and to wonder if they bothered to offer him a little crumb of food and a sup of wine or even a cold glass of water? New Year's Day limps on.

Late afternoon. No visitors have come to the door, no neighbors. No friends or relatives. Red asks if he may go out for a little while and Mother, faltering in the bitter glare from Grandma, says that families should be together on holidays, a remark that makes Red flinch. Grandma tells Mother that her skirt is too God damned short and she'll be talked about behind her back soon if she's not already and her heels are too high and don't look a bit like the Enna Jetticks that Grandpa's hard-earned money is supposed to go to buy! She adds that the next time Mother needs shoes she'll go along with her by Jesus she will. Grandpa is smoking too much, of course, a filthy habit, of course, he's lit the same clipped cigarette three times within the half-hour, that will surely put him at death's door.

There is a knock at the door. A knock? At the door? Friends await without. Relatives and kind acquaintances, smiling neighbors, big-hearted strangers, warmly grumpy fucking old ladies from Hollywood! Red looks over at the ladyfingers and the wine. Grandma puts her finger to her lips and raises her other hand. The knock is repeated, more softly, tentatively, but there is no other sound. Then Father says quietly through the door that he'd like to see Red, he has a little present for him and he'd like to wish them all a happy and healthy New Year if that's not too much to ask. Father says he's as good as sober, he's had just a little hair of the dog, he says that he'd like to see Mother for a minute, he'd like to talk to his wife, or she *was* his wife, to talk to his wife for the love of Christ! Father yells that he'd like Grandma the old bitch to open the door, he dares that henpecked half of a man that she calls a husband to open it, Father bangs heavily on the door and cries out that he prays that God will damn Grandma to Hell forever, the mean coldblooded heartless bitch of a woman who hasn't a particle of a mother's love or kindness in her soul. Then there is silence. Red and Mother, Grandma and Grandpa sit without a sound for ten minutes, then Grandma says in a whisper that she thinks the shiftless drunken sot has gone, the nerve of him on a New Year's Day!

Grandpa says that it wouldn't hurt if they all had a ladyfinger and a glass of sherry about now, to welcome in the year, and so they do. Grandma finishes her sherry and declares that that's enough after such a big meal so late in the day and all the aggravation and that Mother might as well wrap the cakes up and put them away with the bottle too. They can have some more tomorrow, enough is as good as a feast.

Mother opens her mouth, closes it, opens it again, and says that ladyfingers go stale so quick and that Red maybe can have one more? Grandma looks startled, and says that Mother has forgotten all about bread pudding and no wonder worrying about her painted face and the shameless dress she's put on, God only knows for whose benefit.

Bread pudding! Of course, bread pudding! Oh Jesus Christ Almighty! Red feels as if he's choking on buried tears.

Grandma tells Mother to put the God damned ladyfingers away, they've always been the bane of her existence and by God it will be a cold day in Hell that she'll allow them into the house again. Grandpa's New Year's visits and his respects and his old-maid sisters and Aunt Maddy with the first dollar she ever got her claws on sewn into the mattress and all of them afraid to put their noses out the door for fear somebody might look at them crooked is all bad enough, bad enough. Without *this* aggravation over these God damned Protestant cakes. They all want her and they're not to deny it in her grave! Suddenly, Grandma almost jumps out of her chair to run down the hall and fling the door open. Then she slams it shut, locks it, and shuffles back to the dining room.

She grabs Red by his ears and shouts into his face that his Father is a lying mutt as he's left him nothing, nothing at all. Is he surprised? Is he surprised? *Is he surprised?* Mother is wrapping the ladyfingers in wax paper, tears sliding down through the rouge and powder on her face and onto the bosom of her dress. How pretty she looks today, pretty and young, her flesh is warm and sweet, the tramp.

Grandma stares into Red's face and shouts again, something about him not listening to her, not paying any attention to her, as dumb as a post and as stubborn as a mule. She says that we'll soon see how stubborn he is, we'll just see how stubborn, by the Precious Blood of Christ, the brazen little pup!

TWENTY FOUR

❖

Red's final report card reveals, all in glaring scarlet ink, D's and F's in every subject and category of study; in attitude, effort, and deportment. He shows little or no effort, daydreams, talks in class and on line, is uncooperative, has poor conduct, is badly prepared, is lazy. He is a disaster, a perfect example of an educational disaster. The top right corner of the report card shows that he will be promoted, but into 6A-4. Jesus Christ, Jesus Jesus Christ. It would be better to be left back! 6A-4. 6! A! 4! Lock the door on 6A-4. Oh God.

The Rongo brothers, eighteen at least, violent and crazy, maybe they're even twenty. Pulciver the crapshooter who studies only *The Green Sheet*. Big Georgie, who pisses in his pants every day. Dutch, the kid who likes to jump off roofs. Whitey, who is nice and quiet but has to be kept away from little girls. Cheech and his dirty books. There's even some guy in there who stabbed his father. Not to mention the two drunk kids.

The note, addressed to Mother, says, she reads aloud, that he Will Have a Better Opportunity to Learn in this Special Class, that the Class Is a Little Slower and so Affords the Pupils the Time to Learn. It does not say that the Rongo brothers will take turns beating the piss out of him, that Big Georgie will stink up the room, that Whitey will pull up the school idiot, Alice's, dress on the staircase. Of course, if Red Does Well, he Will. Be. Given. Every. Of course. The Rongo brothers! Sweet suffering Jesus.

Grandma is not surprised. She has always known that Red is deviated, thick like his Father, and headed straight down the path to Hell, a path, Grandma says, that is paved with good ideas gone bad. Mother says that she'll go and talk to the teacher, or to the Principal, or to somebody, she doesn't want Red in a class with riffraff and criminal degenerate guineas. She stares at the report card, shaking her head. Grandma is smiling, and says that it will do Red good to be put in his place, maybe it will teach him a lesson and make a real boy out of him instead of a common little thug, who in God's name does he think he is anyway with his swelled head? By the living God, he can barely find his way down to the bin in the cellar! It's lucky for the gawm of a boy that they don't take it into their heads to throw him out of school altogether, like they did to his Father, sixteen years old and in the seventh grade, a disgrace to his ignorant sloven of a mother. Grandma says that she remembers *her* well, a crone of a woman with a wall eye and a chin beJesus that could cut hard cheese, always smelling of sweat and creeping to six o'clock Mass, a lot of good it did her, may she rest in peace. Grandma sighs and says that the unfortunate truth is that Red's Father is not what you would call a mental giant, and now that the midget brain that God gave him has been *destroyed* by cheap rotgut, he can barely tie his own shoes, may God pity the son of a bitch. Let it be a lesson to Red.

Mother says that Red must have done something to get these bad marks, what did he do to get these bad marks? She'll never be able to hold up her head again when people find out that Red is in the stupid class, what did he do to get these bad marks? Mother says that she thought he said he liked Mrs. Meltzer, or that Mrs. Meltzer liked him? Something. Red shrugs and looks down at the floor, blushing as he thinks of the hours he spends trying to see up Mrs. Meltzer's skirt as far as he can when she sits on the desk with her legs crossed, and every wonderfully frustrated minute of every hour a mortal sin. Mother says that she thinks she'll go and talk to her, maybe she'll just put her hat and coat on and go and talk to her, she should damn well go and talk to her and let her see just who Red's Mother *is*, that she's not just some common bohunk that can't speak English. Grandma laughs coldly and says that it will do her not one iota of good to go and talk to a jew schoolteacher, they own the education department in New York lock stock and barrel for Christ's sake, don't the schools come to a halt on Yonkipper, and besides, what will Mother say if this smart jew teacher asks her how come Mother didn't look over Red's homework or didn't see to it that Red got to school on time or had nothing to say when the ignorant boy brought home tests with marks of 20 and 16 and 31 that would shame a black nigger? Hah? Hah!? Grandma says to let sleeping dogs lie and to let the bonehead see what it's like to be among vicious reprobates and sneak thieves and dagos stinking to high heaven of garlic and olive oil. She suddenly turns and smacks Red in the nose with the flat of her hand and as he starts to bleed she tells him not to be grinning like an ape when she's talking. Red covers his nose with a snot-and-semen crusted handkerchief and says that he wasn't grinning really. Grandma tells Mother that she's to stay away from smart-aleck jew schoolteachers who are only too happy to have some shyster lawyer relative sue her for looking at them crooked.

Then some more news. Some days later, Red finds out that Big Mickey is going to be released from reform school again, and that he'll be going to a regular school in the neighbor-hood, he'll be going to Red's school, he'll be, as an authentic thief, malingerer, bully, fighter, and altogether crazy kid, assigned to 6A-4. Of course. Red knows only that Big Mickey is to be released from reform school, but Red *knows*. He thinks of Big Mickey's furious, icy smile and his knees get weak. The Rongo brothers. Big Mickey. And then, a day after this news, Red discovers that Sister Matilda, of the black and terrible eyes, the clawlike grip, the ruthless wooden clappers, the whistling ruler, the abruptly swung Missal, the rosary scourge, Sister Matilda is to teach the sixth and final year of religious instruction class. Red thinks of her as proof that God is always and absolutely *on the job*.

He lies on the couch, looking up into the darkness, listening to the sounds of the wretched world outside the windows. Everywhere, miserable people are hurting each other, lying and cursing and stealing and hitting. They are crying and doing dirty things. The rotten son of a bitches can't help it. Right on the lip of sleep, he wonders, suddenly, how Nancy O'Neill knew that he was going into 6A-4, the little sneak. She kisses all the teachers' asses, a monitor of this and that and every-thing else, hanging around the office after school, dusting and helping out, the little sneak of an asskissing little sneaky bitch. Maybe he *should* have had the moxie to grab her by her box that day at the beach, the crybaby little pill!

Box, box, box. Red just learned this word, a new one that means pussy. But not so dirty. Like you can say it out loud in front of girls, sort of. Box, box. Let me feel your box? Let me feel your box, Nancy? The little sneak, Red kind of likes her.

TWENTY FIVE

❖

One Saturday afternoon when Red gets out of the movies he finds Father waiting for him. For a moment, Red is alarmed. Grandma told him that she never wants him to go to the movies again, no, not if he lives to be a hundred, the movies do him no good and are turning him into a moron degenerate idiot although God knows he doesn't have far to go with the bullet head on him that's a dead giveaway that he's a little thick. But he realizes that Father will say nothing to Grandma, for he has nothing to say to Grandma, and there is no way that she can find out—at least not from Father. But Red knows that Grandma may well find out in other ways because she's a witch. Red knows this.

Red's Father tells him not to look so worried, that he bumped into Mother a couple of days ago and asked her would it be O.K. to treat Red to an ice-cream soda after the movies. Grandma won't know a God damned thing about it if that's what's bothering Red. Red blushes. They are soon in Arnold's ice-cream parlor, sitting at a table in the cool, tile-floored room behind the fountain, Father has a cup of coffee and Red a black and white.

Father tells Red of dogs with their bellies swolled up with poisonous gas, and maggots in prize fighters' water buckets, how blind horses are best for pulling heavy loads but no good for milk wagons, God knows why, it's a mystery, the way to make a cherry bomb blow a window out and not in, yeah, how beautiful Mother was when he met her at an affair at the St. George Hotel where he'll have to take Red swimming once he gets back on his feet, and the wonderful times had by all at Rockaway when he and Mother were keeping company and Grandpa had a little for Christ's sake gumption. Those were the days, uh-huh. Father says that Red probably can't imagine how beautiful a girl Mother was at sixteen, a real Irish colleen, a heartbreaker, and if truth be told, Father wasn't a slouch in the looks department either. Those were the days.

Father says that he saw Rudolph Valentino once right on Court Street outside Joe's, yes, he was with a party of three or four people, all of them dressed to kill, and he says that he still gets looks when he tells people that the great man was a little hop o' my thumb and your typical guinea who looks like a waiter in a pizzaiola restaurant, and that reminds him that he wants to take Red to Joe's where they have about a hundred desserts alone on the menu as soon as he gets straightened out. He says that the police horses that get sick are chopped up to make glue and the stuff that they make bubble gum out of, it's a fact, and that Mother had a very hard time of it when Red was born, some day he'll understand such things, but that Mother and Father wanted more children, a gang of kids, oh well. Father asks Red how he'd like to have a bunch of brothers and sisters like he had. He says that when he was a boy first up was best dressed and best fed, it was hard but fair, hell yes. If anybody dared complain, Red's grandfather would whale them on the bare behind with his razor strop, boys and

girls alike. Father says that Grandma put the hex on the marriage, and believe you me, there's more than meets the eye
there! That little tin soldier of a man, Grandpa, may God take
pity on the likes of him, he knows, oh yes, Grandpa knows,
and some day Red will know because Father will tell him
because Father knows just as Grandpa knows but Mother
doesn't know and it's just as well, let sleeping dogs lie. Father
says that the toughs at CCC camp would eat Big Mickey for
breakfast, and Red laughs, and then laughs harder, eat Big
Mickey for breakfast, and Father laughs too and says and for
lunch too! Father clears his throat and pours some whiskey
into his coffee from a pint bottle of Kinsey Silver Label he
takes from his jacket pocket. He puts his finger to his lips and
winks, then takes a sip.

Father tells Red that the work camps were surrounded by
gangs of girls, tramps mostly, it's not too early for Red to
know that word and a little bit about life so that he can, well,
protect himself, the girls were rotten with disease by and
large, but Father, but Father, well, soon Red will be old
enough to be told about life, and anyway Father became a
priest right after he met Mother, and he laughs as Red's eyes
get wide and he says that he wasn't really a priest but that he
was the nearest thing to a priest, that he was *like* a priest, that
he, well, protected himself for Mother. He says that he bets
that Red can't believe that Mother was so young and beautiful and gay that she'd knock your eyes out, at a dance she was
like the queen bee, not that she's not beautiful still but
nobody is getting any younger. Father says that bloodworms
are the best for bluefish but that when the blues are running
they'll strike at a bare hook, at anything, they go crazy and
the water is nothing but foam and lather when they're feeding
by the thousands, it's a sight you never forget. Father says

that if Red likes he'll take him out on a fishing boat from Sheepshead Bay one of these fine days soon, if Red likes, just the two of them, not Terry, just as soon as Father cleans up some odds and ends. He pours his empty coffee cup halfway full of whiskey and shakes his head. He says that Red should stay away from the sauce, not to follow his example, the rotgut will kill you if you don't go crazy first, he says that it wasn't always this way, there were happy days, believe it or not, happy happy days, he and Mother were as happy as larks together, happy as larks until Grandma, the old bitch, if Red will pardon his French, until the old hag put a hex, a curse, on them both, she never really liked her own daughter, her own flesh and blood, Jesus Christ, and was always jealous of her, yes indeed, jealous of her looks and her personality and that she was full of fun, Grandma's attitude was like she was Mother's older sister, the mean homely sister who is jealous, oh God but they had some good times, a million laughs, of course they had their share of tears and heartaches, but all in all, all in all, it was a good time, all in all, they were happy days, they were so young and full of fun. And then something just went, it just went all to hell, all right, Father was drinking, but that deadbeat clerk guy? Red will know all about it some day, Father says. He says that he once hit six passes in a row shooting crap down by the Navy Yard and then lost all he'd won plus all his pay just like that. Just like that! He says that it was just as well for the wop longshoremen and the squarehead seamen would have cleaned his lamps for him had he won. Just as well. He smiles distantly and lights a cigarette. He says that they made it to his next pay envelope because Mother had saved a little here and there, she was always an angel. He takes a long drag and says that he hopes that Red will stay away from the coffin nails, between them and the booze you've got one foot in the grave.

Father tells Red that you never know, it can happen no matter what, it's a long road that has no turning, time will tell. That a penny saved, a rolling stone, a stitch in time, a face that would stop a clock all have a silver lining. That it's the God's honest truth, it tells no lies, Grandma, the old witch, old bitch, was jealous, everything comes out in the wash. That man proposes but God does something else, creeping Jesus, scared of his shadow, she'd often give him a smile that didn't seem exactly right to him, a smile that was a little fishy, all roads lead to Rome. That it takes broken eggs to be worth a plugged nickel, it's a wise child that knows how to gather moss, a watched pot is always greener, she always insisted on sitting next to him at the dinner table, it's the home of the brave. That a beggar on horseback can tell it to the marines, a bird in the hand makes two wrongs but two in the bush don't make a right, she'd always kiss him before she'd kiss Grandpa on New Year's Eve, oh yes, you can lead a horse to water. That you can't make coals drink, an eye in Newcastle asks no secrets, there was something funny about the way she danced with him at the Shore Road Casino before Red was born when Mother was carrying him, a woman scorned never boils.

Father pours the last of the whiskey into his cup and lights another cigarette. He looks directly at Red and Red sees that his eyes are bloodshot and full of tears. Father says that it was his own fault and he should have had the strength not to be such a God damned fool and that he'll never never never blame Mother for anything. He smiles a ghostly smile and asks Red if he'd like another black and white and Red nods yes. He doesn't want to be here with Father, he doesn't want to listen to Father talk about these things, but he doesn't want to go home and look at Mother or at Grandpa or at Grandma. He'd like to be dead in the Foreign Legion.

Father blows his nose and dabs at his eyes. He says that it's a great life if you don't weaken. Red wishes that the drunk slob of a shanty Irish bastard would just come for him and Mother. He wishes that the fuckprick cockfuck would just come. He wishes that everything that he doesn't want to hurt and break would happen. Would *be*.

TWENTY SIX

❖

Miss O'Reilly loves, protects, and occasionally manages to teach something to the riffraff, trash, flotsam, jetsam, detritus, cripples, and discards that make up class 6A-4. She is a calm, pretty woman of thirty-five, whose straight, slender body, sandy hair in a neat bun, rimless hexagonal glasses, and soft lips enchant Red even as they disturb and inflame him. He doesn't try to look up her skirt when she sits in front of the class to read to them, as he did with Mrs. Meltzer, but, shamefully flustered, he tries to imagine her legs, hidden beneath her prim skirts, amid an incomprehensible welter of lace, silk, elastic, straps, and clasps, and joined at a dark place for which he has no true image. Sometimes Red sweats and blushes with these delicious, crazed visions, and feels as if he is betraying Miss O'Reilly, whose first name, so he discovers, is Alice. Alice O'Reilly, sweet and soft, whose voice is even softer and sweeter than she. Every morning, she tells her misfits that they are as good as anybody else and that they must always hold their heads high. And every morning Sal Rongo clutches his crotch and says that his is about as high as it can get. He and his brother snicker and elbow each other. Miss O'Reilly tells

them that they are not showing the rest of the class any consid-
eration, and she looks directly at Sal, ignoring his obscenity.
Red thinks of Sal falling out the window into the schoolyard,
the jerk. Miss O'Reilly smooths her blouse and skirt, sits at her
desk, and opens her grammar.

Pulciver cannot understand the principles of long division,
fractions, decimals, and many other arithmetical mysteries. He
fails every test that Miss O'Reilly gives, and is unable to complete arithmetic-homework assignments, no matter how short
and simple. In class, he goggles at the blackboard behind his
grotesquely thick glasses whenever she asks him a question.
Hips Ticino says that the only thing Pulciver can add are the
spots on the dice and the class stamps on the floor and yells
with joy as Pulciver turns a deep red and looks at the floor,
blinking. Red feels a little bad for him but what the hell, he's a
dumbbell. A couple of days later, Pulciver tells Red that Miss
O'Reilly is going to make him go over to her house to coach
him in long division and other arithmetic stuff because she's
afraid that he'll get left back. Red laughs and says that if you
get left back in 6A-4 they must throw you in the garbage
dump or the Gowanus Canal, and Pulciver looks alarmed.
Red's heart is sore thinking of Pulciver alone with Miss
O'Reilly. She smells like some kind of flowers.

That afternoon, Red returns after school to the classroom to
find the scarf that he's forgotten, the loss of which will invite a
painful lesson on carelessness from Grandma. As he opens the
classroom door, he sees Miss O'Reilly's lips brushing Pulciver's
who is smiling peacefully up into her tranquil, lovely face. She
turns and smiles at Red and asks him if he's forgotten something. Red, hesitant and flushed, stomps into the wardrobe,
clatters around, and finds his scarf on the floor. Pulciver, with
his disgusting, slobbering, stupid, moron mouth hanging open

and his God damn eyes rolling around like God damn marbles, leaves with Red. As they separate on the street, Red asks him when he has to go put up with the damn extra lessons and Pulciver tells him tonight. This very night the son of a bitch stupid juvenile delinquent will sit next to Miss O'Reilly, alone. All alone with beautiful Alice O'Reilly. Red spits on the sidewalk and says that it's some pain in the ass, he hopes that she won't pick on *him*.

Miss O'Reilly kissing Pulciver, oh sweet Jesus. Tonight she'll kiss him again, she might open her mouth and stick her tongue out like Kenny said they call a soul kiss, she might take her clothes off. She might let the blind dummy look at her thing, look at her, Jesus Christ, pussy. She's in love with Pulciver, kissing him right in the classroom. Red writhes on the couch in the dark, turns and twists until Grandma yells that if he can't lay still, as God is her witness, she'll come in and see if he can lay still for her belt. People can't listen to the radio for the love of God! Red almost yells that he doesn't give a fuck! The world is even worse than Red knows it is, Miss O'Reilly is just a hooer and a tramp like Margie. She's got all her clothes off right now and that son of a bitch Pulciver, he's, he's, that moron Pulciver! She's kissing him and hugging him and he's looking right at her without her clothes on and his eyes are popping out of his head behind his glasses.

On Monday, Miss O'Reilly asks Pulciver to do part of a long-division example on the blackboard and he does it perfectly, then stands blushing and grinning as she puts her arm around his shoulders and tells the class that hard work can accomplish miracles, and that she's only too happy to help the class individually with anything that anybody's having trouble with, they've only to ask her. She squeezes Pulciver's shoulder and he walks back to his desk, still blushing and smiling. Red knows that he's in love with Miss O'Reilly and that Miss O'Reilly is in love with him. The hooer. That night, Red stays awake until it grows light, imagining Miss O'Reilly naked, except that he can't imagine her naked, and he doesn't really want to imagine her naked. He is helpless in his adoration of her and he cries soundlessly into the pillow. The hooer tramp bimbo, just like Margie. The next day he asks Pulciver, wildly, what her pussy looks like, does she have a big bush all over it. Pulciver stares at him, frightened, like the degenerate moron that he is, stares blankly and bewildered.

Red tells Mrs. Meltzer first, then together they go to see the Principal and Red tells him about the kiss and the lesson at home and how she wants to give everybody lessons at home. He feels like vomiting. In the afternoon, Pulciver is called out of class to go to the Principal's office. The next day, Miss Rush, a harsh, hatchet-faced martinet, takes over 6A-4, and tells them that as far as she's concerned they're all hooligans, dolts, and goops and she's not one to mollycoddle anybody, especially little thugs.

At the end of the week, Red passes Miss O'Reilly in the schoolyard. She carries a cardboard box filled with books and papers, pens and pencils, all her school things. Her face is drawn and grey, and as Red walks by, she stops and looks after him. He can feel her eyes on his back, it's terrible. He stops and turns to look at her sweet face. She looks a little bit sick, and he can see that her eyes are wet behind her glasses. She shakes her head slowly and so morosely that Red wants to run over to her and fall at her feet, grovel on the cement, implore her to kick him and beat him and kill him if she wants. Instead, he shouts wildly that he's as stupid as Pulciver, he can't do long division either, he can't spell, he can't do any-thing, he's even stupider than Pulciver! He starts to cry, he whimpers. Oh, Miss O'Reilly! She starts to turn away and he adds that it serves her right, it serves her right, she kissed Pulciver! He watches the beautiful hooer walk away, he watches her beautiful hooer's legs walk away, his bitter world becomes, permanently, more bitter.

TWENTY SEVEN

❖

Red's head is infested with lice and Grandma says that there's no great mystery to it. Lice are always a sign of badness coming out of people, it's a well-known fact. Lice breed in the hair of people who deserve them. She says that it's plain to see that Red likes lice, and vicey-versey, lice like Red. It's the badness in him pure and simple that draws them. She raps him on the skull and pushes him into a chair in the middle of the kitchen and tells him to bend over a basin of scalding water at his feet. She works ashes from the cans on the street into his hair, scouring them, clinkers and all, into his scalp while she recalls that lice are the creatures of the Devil himself along with flies and snakes. God didn't make lice! She rubs his scalp harder, drawing blood with the rough clinkers, and making small sounds of disgust as lice begin to fall into the basin. Grandma says that she wants to get this dirty nigger-work over and done with before Mr. Ginsberg arrives to collect his insurance premium regular as clockwork. God knows that it's a waste of twenty-five cents! What kind of spectacle would it be to let a kike see a woman as refined as Grandma, a woman who has always held her head high and not been ashamed to look any-

one in the eye in spite of her useless daughter, to let him see
her killing lice like some bog-trotter slut such as Red's Father's
common-law tramp? What kind of a spectacle? She deftly
pokes Red in the eye and it begins to water. Grandma says that
he damned well *ought* to cry, bringing shame on his family
with the filth of him!

Red thinks that maybe Mr. Ginsberg, standing patiently,
freeing his accounts book from the thick rubber band that gir-
dles it, might stop Grandma from hurting him. He might crack
Grandma's skull by accident. Set her on fire. Make her slip and
hit her head on the edge of the sink. Yes, your honor, Red says
at the trial, my dear Grandma was shampooing my hair the
way she always does because she loves me so much, to a fault,
and Mr. Ginsberg, the kike, sort of shoved her out the window
by accident. He sobs bitterly in his new suit, with long pants,
and Mother smiles proudly at him as she dabs at her eyes. The
judge says that it's an accident all right and Mr. Ginsberg
won't have to go to jail.

Grandma douses Red's hair with a half-pint of vinegar and
works it into his ashy, blood-streaked scalp. She says that
when she was a girl only the greenhorns just off the boat got
lice, ignorant as sheep, not knowing a thing about a sponge
bath, by God it would make you green around the gills to see
the lice crawling by the dozens from their filthy collars up into
their greasy hair and just as many crawling down from their
hair into the stinking rags of clothes that you could make a
stew out of if you threw them into a pot of boiling water with
an onion and some salt and pepper, it was enough to make an
American girl vomit. But no decent self-respecting Irish boy or
girl born right here ever had so much as a single louse breed
on their heads. It's a sign of badness when they do, badness
inside coming out and no two ways about it. She rubs the vinegar into Red's hair until it starts to get stiff, then pours more

ashes on his head and massages some more. Red's hair is now a thick greyish pudding, and the bodies of scores of lice speckle the surface of the water in the basin. Grandma grabs a handful of Red's gummy coiffure and snaps his head upright. She looks appraisingly and disgustedly at him as she washes her hands at the sink.

Red is sure that this is not all, that this is not enough, that there must be more. Maybe Grandma will stick his head underwater in the bathtub, maybe she'll cook the dead lice in his food, maybe she'll set his hair on fire with kerosene. He waits for Mr. Ginsberg's ring at the door, Ginsberg sent from God to help him, or from the Devil, he doesn't care, Red is lost and damned anyway for his sinful thoughts. Grandma stands in front of him, her hands clasped beneath her apron, upon which is crookedly embroidered the sentiment GOD COULDN'T BE EVERYWHERE THAT'S WHY HE MADE MOTHERS. She has a broad smile on her face, her gold tooth seems especially bright, disaster looms.

Grandma says that she wants Red to go downstairs and sit on the stoop, his hair a loathsome helmet of grey pastelike ashes, flecks of dried blood, and lice, living and dead, all of it stinking of vinegar. Grandma says that air is what his head needs now, fresh air draws the lice out to escape the vinegar, yes. And it won't hurt a bit if people should see him if that's what he's worried about with his long face! Vanity is a sin. Grandma will check on Red from the roof to make sure that he stays right there on the stoop until she calls him to wash his hair, and if he's not on the stoop when she looks, Grandma will beat him within an inch of his life and make him sleep with his hair just as it is and tomorrow he'll have to go out and sit on the stoop anyway. There's nothing like fresh air to bring the lice running out, it's a well-known fact.

Red sits on the stoop. People pass and stare, or laugh, or

shake their heads in horror or sympathy. Those who enter or leave the building shrink away from this grotesque, stinking boy. He imagines Grandma's body falling from the roof and landing in front of him. On the sidewalk. In the gutter. On the hood of a car. In a garbage can. She smacks hard in a gush of blood. No, no. No, no. No, no, no. He's going to Hell.

Sweet Jesus! Red realizes that Big Mickey is standing in front of him, sneering around a cigarette hanging from his mouth. He takes a drag and spits on the sidewalk in front of Red, then shakes his head in pity. He delicately pinches Red's chin with the tips of his fingers and tilts his head up, then blows smoke into his face. He leans close to Red and says that he hears that Red got this case of lice from muff-diving his own Mother, eating his own Mother's dirty pussy, and what does Red have to say to that, is it true? Red, not quite looking at Big Mickey, not quite looking away from Big Mickey, says in a shaking voice that Big Mickey can go and fuck himself and then he can go and fuck his hooer mother and then he can go and fuck his crook of a father for good measure. Red looks across the street placidly. He is in a daze.

Big Mickey steps back. His smile is weirdly frozen, calm and bloodthirsty, the smile of Pretty Boy Floyd, Baby Face Nelson, Machine Gun Kelly, Clyde Barrow, John Dillinger, Al Capone. He says that he can hardly believe his ears, he says dear oh dear, he says well well well. Red waits for the first terrible blow as a dying louse crawls slowly toward his eyebrow.

TWENTY EIGHT

❖

Anything that disturbs Grandma's fragile composure is ultimately the fault of Red, the lout, the miscreant, the ungrateful: he on whom charity is wasted, he who is rotten to the very core.

When Grandma makes her egg too soft and runny, she strikes Red so hard that he shits himself. When Grandma's corset makes it difficult for her to breathe, she cuffs Red on the nape of the neck so violently that he pisses his pants. Should Grandma unexpectedly come face to face with a priest or nun she smacks Red until he bleeds from the ears. If Red becomes terrified when Grandma summons the demon, Hurley Lees, by thrice intoning, Hurley Lees, come blow your horn, the king's son is in your garden, she contemptuously knocks him on the sconce till his eyes rattle. Should it occur that a story in the *News* of seduction and immorality among the rich and celebrated titillates Grandma, she whacks Red so that snot flies out of his nose. When Grandma bitterly considers that Grandpa no longer cares to see her naked, she bashes Red's ribs until he begs for mercy. Should the thought cross her mind of Red's drunken Father forcing her to foxtrot with him at the

Shore Road Casino, Grandma repeatedly bangs Red on one side of the head and then the other until he finally crawls on his hands and knees. When she recalls her sister getting her hands on their late mother's dinner ring, Grandma thumps Red in the kidneys until he writes in agony. If the hand-me-downs that Mother often wears make her into a dowdy embarrassment, Grandma thwacks Red's solar plexus so forcefully that he pukes all over himself. If Grandma makes roast leg of lamb too dry, she punches Red's face until he screams. Should Mother anger Grandma by suggesting that she go to Confession, Grandma buffets Red till he cries like a baby. If memories of sexual intercourse with Grandpa arouse her, Grandma slaps Red so silly that his knees buckle. When Grandma recalls beating cousin Katy with belt, stick, ruler, and cane, her guilt is such that she swats Red with a broom hard enough to break his back. When her nightly consumption of beer makes Grandma drunk, she bludgeons Red's buttocks until he comes. If a Dodgers' victory makes Grandpa happy, Grandma clubs Red so viciously that spittle sprays from his mouth. If Grandma should see Mother in her underwear and recognize that her daughter's body is still attractive, she smites Red until he weeps blood. When Grandpa temporarily switches to 20 Grands so that he may buy more cigarettes with money saved, Grandma spanks Red with a spatula so that he screeches like a cat. If Phil the butcher gives Grandma tough or fatty meat, she thrashes Red while he squirms on the floor. Should men ogle Mother on the street, Grandma beats Red until he shakes with fever. When it occurs to Grandma that Mother and Grandpa may outlive her, she swats Red across the face until he blithers like an idiot; and when it then occurs to Grandma that she may outlive Mother and Grandpa, she pastes Red in the mouth so that he again blithers like an idiot. Should Grandma feel old when men on the street don't ogle

Mother, she conks Red between the eyes until he shakes with
fever. If Phil the butcher gives Grandma especially lean and
tender meat, her surprise is such that she bops Red with a wet
mop as he squirms on the floor. When Grandpa switches to 20
Grands, a niggerguinea cigarette, Grandma crowns Red with a
skillet so that he screeches like a cat. Should Grandma glimpse
Mother in her underwear and notice that her daughter's body
is beginning to sag, she clips Red with her fist until he weeps
blood. If Grandpa is sullen because of a Dodgers' loss,
Grandma socks red so furiously that spittle sprays from his
mouth. Should Grandma, after a night of beer-drinking,
remain sober, she clouts Red's buttocks with such vigor as to
make him come. When Grandma recalls her abuse of cousin
Katy with hanger, wooden slat, ladle, and switch, she feels
such joy that she clobbers Red with a potato masher so that
his back seems almost to break. When memories of sexual
intercourse with Grandpa intrude themselves on Grandma, she
feels such disgust that she wallops Red so that his knees
buckle. If Grandma even considers going to Confession, she
feels such terror that she cudgels Red with a barrel stave until
he cries like a baby. If Grandma makes roast leg of lamb too
pink, the threat of ptomaine poisoning so unnerves her that
she belts Red with a wooden spoon until he screams. If
Mother looks attractive in the shabby hand-me-downs that she
must sometimes wear, Grandma lambastes Red with anything
that comes to hand so that he pukes all over himself. When
Grandma looks at the tiny diamond-chip brooch that is all she
got of her late mother's things, she whips Red until he writhes
in agony. Should Grandma recall Red's tipsy Father whirling
her delightfully around the dance floor of the Hamilton
House, she flagellates Red until her arm is weary and he is
crawling on his hands and knees. If Grandma realizes that she
is pleased that Grandpa no longer cares to see her naked, she

belabors Red with kitchen implements until he begs for mercy. When stories in the *News* of seduction and immorality in Hollywood disturb and anger Grandma, she lashes Red until snot flies out of his nose. Should Grandma's invocation of the demon, Hurley Lees, produce but indifference or contempt in Red, she scourges him with the buckle end of Grandpa's belt until his eyes rattle in his head. Should Grandma be approached by a priest or nun on the street, she flogs Red so that he bleeds from his ears. If Grandma's corset makes her feel lumpy and unattractive, she batters Red so relentlessly that he pisses his pants. When Grandma makes her egg too hard and dry, she pummels Red until he shits himself.

The thug, the fiend, the malcontent: he who will come to a bad end.

TWENTY NINE

❖

The new teacher of the 6A-4 rabble is Miss Crane, a horrifyingly thin woman with hair of a startling tomato red. She has some difficulty in controlling the class, but does as well as might be expected. Red likes the way her dresses hang pathetically from the jagged angles of her bony body and the way she squeezes her eyes shut and clasps her hands together when Big Mickey or one of the Rongos spits on the floor or suddenly breaks something. At these moments, she seems like a helpless girl a scientist has captured for some experiment. She also has endearing twitches, and she coughs and clears her throat obsessively.

Miss Crane has a belief in the practice of writing compositions, and considers it a prescription for educational, ethical, moral, and mental ills: she trembles and hacks wildly as she tells the wretched pupils of the joys of writing well. She assigns a composition a week, and so as to allow the class to boost each other up, as she puts it, everyone must write on the same subject at the same time. Miss Crane's subjects are diverse, from Fun in the Summertime to Making Friends with the Grocer, but may be reduced to three major themes: pets, family, friends.

Red likes to write these compositions, even though his orga-
nizing abilities are virtually hopeless, and his spelling, grammar, and syntax never improve. Yet his unwavering conception
of the mean world and his talents for mendacity find a perfect
locus in the small sagas that he writes in a kind of distant stupor.

C–. Very interesting. Miss Crane's elbow pokes sharply into
her sleeve.

Red writes of his little Scoty that he raised from a pup that
jumped out the window and flew a few feet until he dyed a
paneful death hiting the closeline man in the court yard and
then bounce on a pickett fense, of the wonderful pals he use to
have when he lived in the cuntry when his Father was a farmer,
of his Mother, the beautyful actress who is now deaf and
dumm and a crippel it is a trajady. He tells of Rex and Prince
the poliece dogs that a snake ate down in the cellar bins and of
the rich kid he met at a party on Park Avenue who had lep-
rosey even though his father owns a Bank it gos to show you
and how his Grandpa once had a casuel chat with Hubert
Hoover the Head of the Depresion. Then there is the milkmans
horse who likes to ate his joly Grandmas' delacacy headcheese,
his Boy scout pals that he will soon join who have neckacheifs
with frankfooters in camping, and his Father inventing a new
mashine for the Defense effort. He speaks about Rollo the dog
who could talk in a saloon and once told a joke about a dog
who could talk in saloons, of the neat kid he met in the play-
ground who dyed from tomane ice cream and came back to
Life when his mother litt a candle after the Benediction, and of
his Grandma taking him to Steeplechase and Luna park even
though of her clubfoot. There was a crab about as big as a
water rat that followed a kid all the way home that he knows
from the 69 street peer and the kid was running, there was a
boy he knew from release time religion class with a dirty book

and he went blind also his hands fell off, and his Father has a little boat in Sheepsead bay cristened Margie after his mutt dog.

C–. Very interesting. Miss Crane reaches for her Carstairs and water.

Red tells the astonishing story of the mouse that would not dye though it was cut in a half. He recalls the bully that fell in betwen a scow and the peer and his gutts came right out of his mouth after he socked a girl in her private place. He confides that his cousin Katys husband used to be mayer of Union city Jersey till he fell off a trolley whose door that opened by a nigger he is now a crippel.

C–. Very interesting. Miss Crane lights a Herbert Tareyton.

The canarye Red owns that can sing oh my darling Clementine and barnacle Bill the sailer that his Grandpa taught and who likes a puff of ciggarette and some Wilsons' from a shotglass. The kid he knew whos mother could not be buryed in Holy ground since she was a Protessunt and he foam at the mouth. His poor Mother whos cheeks are still rosy pink that his dear Grandma takes in a wheel chair with her bum foot every day to look at the Bay in the park. What about the praying Mantiss that it costs 40 dolars fine if you kill it because it eats Japonese beetles and rubish and the secret gang who burn you with a ciggarette on 69 st. if you're not a ginnie and the giant Christmas tree that his Grandpa goes up to the woods to chop down with his Buick? And the animals in the Zoo in Prospec park all remember Red you can allways tell with a wild animals' roar. Red has many many freinds surround him but most of them are chumps and he does not have time to waste for chumps because Life is short. That is what Red's Father like to say as he invents a mashine gun for the U S army of America. And the Champion St. Bernodd dog that they owned for many years that won 20 Blue ribbens ate a poi-

soned rat with J-O roach paste and drowned himself in the toilet, and a good pal of Reds' tried to do something funny with a
girl and fell off the ferriss wheel just an hour later after the
Tunnel of love and his Miracleous medal in his hand burned
right through his hand, and also just last night Reds beloved
Grandma got knocked off the platform on DeKalb ave and
crushed to death by the Sea Beach express and the wake is
tonight and it is a real hart braking thing.

C–. Very interesting. Miss Crane says that maybe Jesus
Christ in His infinite mercy, maybe Jesus Christ. She starts to
laugh in nervous frenzy, twitching, trembling, convulsively
jerking back and forth on a chair in the ferocious light of her
kitchen.

THIRTY

❖

Grandma parts the drapes that separate the dining room from the front room and looks intently into Red's face to see if he is sleeping. Red is not sleeping. He is flying high above the Barren Wastes, the Trackless Sahara, the Graveyard of Hope, snug in the tiny cockpit of the Hornet, his crack biplane. Grandma peers steadily at Red but he is a master of treachery and his dull face is in perfect repose. Grandma lets the drapes fall back into place, steps backward into the dining room, and says that the useless lump is asleep, although she'd be perfectly content to let him hear her say her piece to Mother, there's not a lot that gets by the little sneak anyway. Red says silently to the ceiling that the old bitch is half-polluted already. He pulls up sharply at the crack of a bloodthirsty Arab's rifle, you can never trust the swarthy heathen devils!

Grandma says that it's immaterial to her and to Grandpa, the damn fool of a hardworking slob just to keep a crumb of food on the table for the two of them, let alone Mother and Red, so if Mother thinks that Grandma would not be ready willing and able to pack her and her hooligan son off to Katy's in Jersey she'd better think again. Then they'd see, the two of them, the prima donnas, what it's like to live with a woman who puts newspapers on the floor so nobody will, God save us, put a scuff on the pitiful linoleum that's been down ever since linoleum was invented and a woman who runs into the bathroom after somebody's done their business to give it a scrubbing, by Jesus Christ's Own Precious Blood it's enough to make a regular American who wasn't born in the gutter puke up their guts, and then there's her gawm of a crippled husband, God bless the mark, all twisted up like a pretzel in his easy chair, nodding his head and listening to the serials, Stella something, and everything else, all day and all night, with the spit dropping out of his mouth like some paddy who's after drooling all down himself at a wake in his mad lunge for the whiskey as long as it's free, and every once in a while the pitiful man pisses his pants to break the monotony. By God, if Mother thinks that Grandma won't be happy to send her and Red straight across the river on the tubes so fast it will make their heads spin she's got another think coming, yes she has. Grandma says that she's fed up with her complaints.

Red spots a girl who looks like, who might be, who *is* Joanne Carman, trapped in a Cave of Terror by a giant gorilla and a boacun stricter and her soft beautiful mouth is open in a scream and her dress is ripped down the front, no, she's lost her dress, she's cringing there screaming in some kind of thing with lace or her slip, her beautiful hands crossed on her beautiful chest to hide her beautiful little bosom swelling up under the silk stuff, and her beautiful legs are bare except for her white knee socks that are in tatters because of the sharp thorns of the Forbidding Wilds. Red lands on a dime! That's that for the boacun stricter, his head is gone with a single stroke of Red's silver blade. That's that for the giant gorilla, Red lets some daylight into him with his well-oiled carbine. Joanne Carman is crying with happiness but she is also ashamed that she is in her beautiful slip, with her beautiful bosom showing through a little, and her beautiful bare legs. She blushes as red as a beet and her eyes are cast down. Red pretends not to look at her shyness since he is not a two-bit scumbag.

Oh yes indeed, if Mother thinks she has too much to do around here, too much to *do!*—Grandma laughs in a ragged terrible falsetto. Red hears the dull sound of a full glass of beer set down on the card table. Grandma says to Grandpa that if Mother thinks she has too much to *do* she has some half-assed notion of what too much to *do* is, and Grandpa says that Mother has no notion of what too much to do *is*, and Grandma says that if Mother wants to find out what too much to do really *means*, and Grandpa repeats that if Mother wants to find out what too much to do *really* means, Grandma concludes by saying that Katy will be only too God damned glad to show her. *And* show her lazy shiftless bum of a son, who is well on his way to winding up in the penitentiary, where to get off. Grandpa says that as the twig is bent the tree will break. Grandma says that Red was always bad, always wild, but that there was a spark of decency in the boy, at least one. little. spark. of decency. Christ knows that people had to look for it, but give the Devil his due, it was there. Grandpa says that the boy was not all bad, that there *was* a spark of decency in him. He recalls how Red would go down to the bin in the cellar to get things for Grandma with never a word out of him. He even learned to keep a civil tongue in his head. Grandma laughs and says that he had to be whipped and welted to learn how to be a boy, a real boy, but she's not shy when it comes to discipline and she can still teach a lesson when needed, there's nothing like a good crack in the face to make a child know its place. Grandpa says that a crack in the face never did a bit of harm to anybody, look at Mother. Grandma suddenly shouts that it and more may be needed soon because by bloody Jesus on the

Cross the lummox of a boy is turning into some kind of a criminal lout! He was bad enough before he was put into that terrible class for guineas and morphodites and jailbirds from the reform school and the worst sort of riffraff with their polluted blood and even some kike or arab of a dice shooter, oh she's heard what she's heard, and it's a miracle that they don't put a couple of niggers in the class, by God they'd fit right in with the dese dems and dose hoodlums and burglars, and she wouldn't put it past them. Grandma says that Red is heading straight for the penitentiary and he'll arrive there diseased rotten in body and mind, shaking like a leaf with some dirty sickness, old before his time. She says that she'll not stand for it, it's time somebody put their foot down, she'll be damned to Hell if she'll stand for a bullet-headed idiot of a boy who spends all his time with a long face on him lording it all over everybody, and will Mother look at her poor slave of a father, will she look at him? Grandma will not have the poor man putting up with somebody who hobnobs with niggers or just as bad!

There's not much room in the Hornet for two people, so Joanne Carman has to sit on Red's lap as he zooms through the blue, showing her the Emerald Jungle below so that she can thrill to the Thundering Beauty of the waterfalls and the Shadowy Lairs of the silent panther and mighty lion, King of Beasts. Red puts his leather jacket and white silk scarf on her so that the icy air of the open skies won't make her catch her death of cold, and she snuggles against him. He does some expert daredevil loops and tailspins and she looks at him and says that it's hard to believe that he's in 6A-4 with the stupid greaseballs and feebs, and Red colors and says that it's all a mistake they made in the office, soon he'll be in the right class. Joanne Carman settles into Red's lap and turns so that he can look into her beautiful brown eyes and see her beautiful soft mouth and she throws a beautiful arm around his neck and leans so close that he can smell her warm beautiful breath that's like mint and flowers and oranges. She whispers that maybe Red will be put into *her* class and he can feel the warmth and softness of her beautiful bottom on his thighs through her beautiful slip.

Grandma says that maybe Mother would *prefer* to work like a slave at Katy's, and see Red swallow her iron discipline, more, much more, than he ever has to put up with *here*, God knows, neither she nor Grandpa have the energy anymore, no, Mother is not to look at her as if she's crazy, Grandma can feel old age creeping up and Grandpa's not getting any younger. Grandma says that although she does her best to chastise Red she just doesn't have the energy. When she gives him a little slap in the face he looks at her as much as to say that she can kiss his royal ass, oh yes, excuse the expression, but that's what the ungrateful little pimp means to say, as God is her judge. Or maybe Mother thinks that she can raise Red all by herself in her own apartment, if she had a job so that she could afford an apartment, and that's not likely, what with her being away from the business world for so long, besotted as she was like some cheap little chippie with Red's Father, a man who never, on his best day, had two nickels to rub together. And Mother can't be looking for a handout from Grandma and Grandpa, she thinks they're made of money anyway, poor Grandpa working like a slave a dog a nigger a bohunk a sheeny peddler a greenhorn just off the boat with a cardboard valise. And for what? For Red to insult him by telling every Tom Dick and Harry who will listen that his Grandpa drinks? Grandma knows, oh yes, she hears the stories, she hears plenty about what comes out of the little thug's mouth. But, *but* if Mother wants to shake the dust of her own mother and father off her feet and see if she can fend for herself and her useless

son, who is a hair's breadth away from the inside of the nearest police station, well then, good luck to her, there's nobody
who will try to stop her. Nobody can ever stop a born tramp
anyway from doing what she damn well pleases. Grandma
says that maybe Mother will bump into some new boyfriend, a
new boyfriend is all she needs, Jesus Mary and Joseph, it was
the *old* boyfriend, some horse's ass with his Howard suits, that
patch on a man's ass, who drove Father out of his own house
and into the street and to the hard liquor at last, not that he
isn't a weakling with his harebrained get-rich-quick schemes
and his common slut of a new *wife*, don't make Grandma
laugh! Grandma hopes that Mother is satisfied. Mother says
oh God oh God oh God oh God oh God help her, what has
she ever done in her life to deserve this, and Grandma laughs
that it's not God who can help her, and that she should have
thought of God when that namby-pamby skirt chaser came
sniffing around *her* skirts with his bookkeeper's face and no
chin, buying her underwear and candy, Grandma knows, it
was enough to make a decent woman hang her head in shame.
Grandma says that God wasn't given a thought when Mother
put on her black nightgowns, oh yes, don't stare, or sat in a
barroom till all hours drinking Tom Collins with her legs
crossed on a stool and a cigarette in her gob like a common
streetwalker.

Joanne Carman says that maybe he can *ask* to be in her
class so that they can see each other every day, and Red can
walk her home, she lives in Flagg Court, Red knows where
that is, doesn't he? Red says that of course he does, that's the
big fancy apartment house with the fountain and the iron
gates, and Joanne Carman says that there is also a pool for res-
idents' entertaining pleasure. She colors a little and says that
maybe she and Red can go swimming and that she'd like him
to see her new bathing suit that she and her mother bought at

A&S, it's a sunflower yellow with cunning little powder-blue flowers on the, and she gestures toward her beautiful bosom and flutters her eyelids and looks down. Red feels her warmth on his lap, her head is on his shoulder, burning with girlish shame, and Red says oh Jesus, oh boy, oh Jesus Christ Almighty, and Joanne Carman is shifting on his lap to beat the band.

Grandma says that what Red needs is a little less coddling and the gumption to get himself out of that class for degenerates, that's the first thing. By God, they can't even keep the same teacher with that bunch of wild Indians. She says that they're all animals, but what can anybody expect from dagos and dinges and Christ knows what class of lowlife they throw in there like rubbish. She sighs drunkenly and says that they all need the strap.

Red says oh Joanne, oh Joanne. He bites the sheet and blanket as he falls into the dizzy world of love. Joanne Carman is astride him, he lets go of the controls, the Hornet goes into a steep dive toward the Brooding Congo. They'll both be killed and their bodies found locked together in an Embrace of Death!

THIRTY ONE

❖

Red asks Whitey if it's true that they were going to put him away in the Kings County crazy house if he kept on fooling around or whatever he did with little girls, and Whitey grins warmly and beautifully and says that the girls weren't all so little and that they liked what he did, all girls are really hooers anyway and wind up drunk all night in saloons, most of them do anyway. Red says that he can't even imagine going up to a girl he likes and asking her to do something, uh, something funny. He says that he can't even imagine asking a girl to take a walk. Whitey puts his hands in his pockets and raises his chin delicately so that the sunlight slanting into the schoolyard falls across his soft, pretty face. He says that you got to kill a cat, it's a cinch to get girls if you kill a cat. Red looks at him, his mouth slightly open in wonder and in hope. He says that you have to kill a cat? Whitey says that that's the ticket all right, you kill some fucking cat and you can do as you please with girls, they're in your power, sort of, they're, like they like it. Red says that he can't believe that some jerk, like Sal Rongo maybe, could get a girl with *fifty* dead cats, but Whitey nods his head and says that even a bum like Sal could get whatever he wants but that he'd never tell Sal about the cats because he's a stupid wrong-o who likes to push little guys around and some day Whitey is going to clean his clock for him good. Red says that what? you just kill a cat? any way you like? Whitey says that that's what you do, you kill the little bastard and you have a charm over girls, you don't have to mention it or anything, it's just there.

Red thinks about this for a few days, about Georgene Marshall and Mary Ryan and Inez Hanlon, Constance Piro and Gladys Heffernan, all standing in a row taking their dresses off like the hooers that Whitey says they all are. Whitey says that even his mother is a hooer and she's the one wanted to put him in Kings County, sure, so she could bring home guys from the saloon and not have to worry about him being around. Whitey says that they're all like that, they're all dirty hooers underneath.

Red has his eye on a cat that always hangs around the cellar where Black Tom, the super, lives. It's thin and mangy, with a deep gouge over one eye where fur won't grow, a badly shredded ear, and yellow crusted eyes. Red figures that this is the cat to kill, this diseased, useless animal that nobody cares about, even Black Tom kicks it out of his way at every opportunity, and Grandma calls Black Tom human garbage. One Friday, Red asks the fish peddler for some guts and tails and gets a handful in a piece of newspaper. Then he walks through the lots until he finds a rock about the size of a baseball. He nods to himself that the God damned cat is dead already. Mary Ryan, Gladys Heffernan, Mary! Gladys! They say that they've always really liked Red a lot and they blush and giggle, Jesus.

Red finds the cat stretched out in the sun at the top of the cellarway stairs. He says that the kitty is a good kitty a nice kitty a pretty kitty a good kitty kitty, and he holds out the newspaper bundle smoothly. The cat is wary but the odor of

fish is so irresistible, so astonishing, that as Red backs down
the steps, the offering held at arm's length, the cat rises,
stretches, and limps after him, favoring a foreleg cut and caked
with dried blood. Red says that the cat is a filthy, lousy, pretty
kitty, pretty dead kitty, and then turns at the foot of the stairs,
walks into the gloom of the cellarway, turns again, opens the
sopping newspaper bundle, and lays it on the cement floor.
The cat loses all caution, and crazed with hunger, rushes to the
bloody mess and begins to eat furiously. Red bashes its skull
open with the rock, then bashes it again for good measure.
The cat twitches and trembles, its forelegs straight before it,
blood from its skull pouring onto and mixing with the bloody
offal. But the son of a bitch is still alive! One eye stares
cloudily up at Red, the other is occulted by the gore of its mortal wound.

Red raises the rock again but cannot bring it down on the
wretched animal, the sound of the two crushing blows lodged
heavily in his ears. Instead, he abruptly, desperately, almost
deliriously seizes the cat's throat in his red, sticky, fishy fingers
and chokes it to death. The cat's eye remains on him through
the silent, dreamy killing, an eye full of what seems to Red
some terrible dirty knowledge about something, about girls?
Red says to the corpse that pretty soon he'll be pulling down
Connie Piro's pants, maybe he'll pull down Mrs. Meltzer's
pants, Whitey's right that they're all a bunch of hooers, you
mangy bastard.

The butchered cat is the subject of neighborhood gossip for
a day or two, and almost everybody is of Grandma's opinion,
that Black Tom, that pitiful harp who gives a bad name to the
Irish just by drawing breath, flew into a murderous rage and
thanks be to God that some sweet clean girl from O.L.A.
wasn't in his clutches. There's not much that Grandma'd put
past Black Tom, a man who lives in his stinking clothes day in

and day out and has the first nickel he ever made, God only knows why the police don't give the gawm a regular beating on general principles.

Red dreams that Grandma is in a dark hallway with a bag that oozes and drips blood, she says that a bag is full of coconut buns that Red likes and that he can have all he wants, Mother reaches into a bag and takes out a bright red coconut that is a rock, Red turns at a sound in the kitchen and Miss O'Reilly is there and touches him between his legs, her belt hangs from her hand for she's whipped Red's dead cat, she rubs and fondles him luxuriously, Red says that she's a hooer and he's wise to her, he looks down and there are bleeding cats swarming at his feet, Miss O'Reilly says to Grandma that Red is much too cruel for her class, she's very sorry, she'd love to let him feel her up but it's too bad, it's just too bad, Grandma laughs girlishly and whispers that there's no finer sight than a jew teacher putting on airs, and Red says that he will marry her, he grins vacuously as his body is sweetly overwhelmed by sweetest pleasure, a cat, Red will kill a million of them.

THIRTY TWO

❖

Mother is out early one Saturday morning looking for work in what Grandpa calls the restaurant field, he says that they're always on the lookout for peppy janes, neat as a pin, in the restaurant field, gals who can wait tables, handle the counter lunch trade, work the steam table. He looks serious, somber, and immediately after so arranging his expression, says that no matter how tough things may be, although, thank God, with the war overseas business is picking up at last, no matter how tough, people have to eat. He pauses, nods his head, and says that people, yes indeed, have to eat no matter what the times are like, good bad or indifferent. People. Have. To. Eat.

On Saturday mornings, Grandma always discovers many small chores for Red to do or errands for him to run, in the unspoken hope that they'll take up so much time that he'll be unable to make the matinee at the Alpine, or, if he does arrive in time for the main feature, he'll miss the cartoons, the specialties, the latest chapter of *Daredevils of the Red Circle*, the free comic book, and the bag of stale candy. Mother, however, helps Red to perform these chores, most often doing the odds and ends of shopping that Grandma suddenly remembers must be done. Saturday mornings comprise elaborately ritualized demonstrations of thrust and counterthrust by Grandma and Mother, performed with never a word as to their real intentions and meanings: all is almost blithely disingenuous. Grandma's icy smile pretends that the tasks are—unfortunately!—necessary to existence; Mother's fixed look of alertness assumes that Grandma understands that a mother's role is to aid her son, who is, of course, a grandmother's beloved and cherished grandson. On this particular morning, Grandma has the luxury of toying with her prey. It's a near certainty that not only will Red miss the best part of the matinee, he'll be forced to accept Grandma's excoriations of the pissabed shopkeepers, kikes, and dagos who would steal the pennies off a dead man's eyes, as those responsible.

Almost as soon as the door closes behind Mother in her carefully brushed, shabby tweed coat and little green felt hat, Grandma says that she wants Red to run a few errands for her. She smiles weirdly in what she guesses is a friendly way, and adds that Red can keep whatever change is left, so that he can buy himself some candy: Candy to eat: All by himself: At the matinee! Red looks at Grandma with a meticulously neutral look and smiles uncertainly, noncommittally. The sense that a pit is opening behind him, one into which he will be casually pushed at the right moment, comes over him. Grandma says that he won't mind having a few pennies to spend on himself, will he, he won't mind having some money, maybe even a nickel, to keep his pocket warm, will he, he won't mind having some root beer barrels or licorice or red hots to chew on while he's *enjoying the matinee*, will he! Red shakes his head no and says that it sounds neat and thanks Grandma. Ah, the pit gapes wider and deeper.

Grandma tells Red to go to the guinea greengrocer and then the bakery right down the street with the washed out Bible-

thumper of a girl with thick glasses behind the counter, Red
knows who she means. She wants two nice ripe tomatoes from
the guinea's and three hard rolls with poppy seeds from the
bakery, that's all she wants. She gives Red some money and
says that it ought to be plenty and with a penny or two left
over. She beams savagely. The change will be Red's! When Red
returns with these things Grandma has on an almost tragically
worried face, a face that Red instantly recognizes as spectacu-
larly insincere. Grandma says that she's sorry, but she forgot
that she needs a pound of chuck chopped from Phil the
butcher, but that Red should still have plenty of time to get to
the Alpine like all the other boys who never think of helping
out at home the way Red does. Grandma says that she sin-
cerely hopes so. Her concern is so stunningly false and yet so
brilliantly presented that Red almost laughs. But he does not
laugh, for that would unfailingly preclude the matinee: it *is*
still possible that he'll get to the Alpine on time, but Red has
little hope of this. He sees in the forgotten chuck chopped the
sign of the master strategist, and all he can do is watch the
campaign unfold and prepare to submerge all traces of anger.

Grandma gives Red some more money to add to the six
cents he has left, and he leaves. Upon his return, Grandma is
sitting morosely at the kitchen table, her eyes almost brimming
with tears. Red stands stunned. Tears! It staggers him to realize that Grandma is truly embarked upon a full-scale assault.
TEARS! Grandma looks over at him, points to the tomatoes
and the rolls in turn, to the pathetic still life they form on the
table. She says that she should have known better than to send
poor thick Red to stores where you can't trust them to take
pity on a boy who's a little slow and in the special class at
school with the pitiful morphodites. Not only don't the riffraff
guineas and God damn jumping Baptist holy rollers have an
ounce of pity, they go out of their way to take advantage of a

boy who is as good as a moron, may God forgive her, honesty
has always been one of Grandma's faults, but she means no
harm, as God is her judge. There is nothing to do but send Red
back to the blackhearted ginzola with his filthy hands and take
his soft, rotten tomatoes back to him with a note, by Jesus,
telling him where to get off, and send Red back to the dried-up
old maid with the glasses on her like telescopes, and take the
rolls that are not what anybody would have the nerve to call
fresh and where are the poppy seeds, does she call this pitiful
little sprinkle poppy seeds? She'll get a note too, the stingy
Swede. Grandma says that she wants her money back and by
God she'll get it back every penny of it or she'll see what's
what! Red carelessly glances over at the kitchen clock, there's
still time, even with this new errand. His eyes meet Grandma's
for a moment and he knows that she's seen his thoughts. He
puts on an idiot face, mouth hanging open, takes the tomatoes,
the rolls, and the notes, and leaves.

The small portion remaining of the morning is absorbed by
Grandma's relentless astonishment at how ill-served she is by
the neighborhood merchants and by her redress of these injus-
tices. Red returns to the apartment to find that the chuck
chopped from Phil is not fresh, no, it's rotten, it's from the tray
that's been left out all night, does the insolent man think that
she was born yesterday? The swill must be returned with an
especially harsh note. Grandma looks, abashed, at the roof
outside the kitchen window, and *blushes*. She says that she's
forgotten to ask Red to drop into Dreyer's for a minute for a
quarter pound of farmer cheese from the fat nazi as long as
he's taking back the chuck chopped, she says that Red is so
good to give up his Saturday morning like this that she's happy
that she'll be giving him whatever change is left, it's the least
she can do.

The fat sauerkraut-lover of a nazi hun has the *nerve* to give an American boy like Red farmer cheese that might have been fresh when Napoleon was a cadet, the disgusting bunder or whatever they call themselves with a picture of Hitler on the wall in the back of the store looking like something the cat dragged in with a moustache on him like a little smear of shite. Grandma is sorry about this, she knows it's late, it looks as if, well, if Red hurries, if he *really* hurries, he might, let's hope so, Grandma says that never say die is her motto. Red stares at her because he suddenly remembers that Mother always says that Grandma's motto is don't open the door. Grandma says that Red has to take this stinking farmer cheese back to the nazi.

Red appreciates Grandma's malevolent genius, for Dreyer's is directly across the street from the Alpine. Grandma, in a triumph of timing, has so arranged it that as Red approaches the delicatessen, the turbulent, noisy, raucous line of kids outside the theatre is being admitted. Too late. Of course it's too late. Red hands the package and the note to Mr. Dreyer, and watches him read, his lip curling in contempt. He opens the cash register, slams some change into Red's hand, and says that he can tell his Grandma that she can shopping go to some other store if she thinks his farmer cheese is fit for the pigs. His round face is red and swollen and Red stays for a few seconds feigning stupid surprise, in the hope that the kraut son of a bitch might drop dead of a stroke.

When he arrives back in the apartment, Grandma says that it looks as if he might miss a little of the matinee, does it matter? She says that it serves him right anyway, since he's such a slowpoke and since because no matter how many times Grandma tells him, he *never looks* at what he's buying and so the thieves of shopkeepers walk all over him. He just *never looks!* Red says nothing and Grandma, narrowing her eyes, says that whether Red wants to go to the Alpine or not, matinee or no matinee, he has to eat lunch first, oh yes, she's not letting him out of the house without lunch with all of the sickness that's going around, that's all she needs, Red sick, then she'll be a nurse as well as the chief cook and bottle-washer. Grandma pauses, thinking, and Red sees her take a breath and say that there'll be no change for candy because, well, Grandma didn't buy a thing! *No change*. She simpers chillingly.

Red sits at the table. He says that that's fine. He says that everything is O.K. He says that maybe he's getting a little too old for matinees anyway, with all the little kids screaming. Grandma says that that's what she thinks and she's happy to see that he's got a head on his shoulders. She says that there's no reason for him to go to the Saturday matinees anymore at all. There's a small fleeting suggestion, a passing hint of a smile on Grandma's face. He can stay home and help her and Mother and Grandpa with a million things. Red says that by the way he just remembered that Mr. Dreyer said to be sure to tell Grandma that he thinks she's a filthy dog. Or a dirty pig. Red forgets.

THIRTY THREE

❖

Grandma and Mother, together and singly, nudge, lecture, and harangue Grandpa on the need for him to be more of a *real* father to Red. Their motives are quite different, but they are in agreement that Red's failures in school, his disgusting lack of concern for personal hygiene, his slack-jawed leer, his increasingly foul mouth, and his attraction to the sort of friends that look like something the cat dragged in, are the result of having a Father who is an adulterous drunken layabout of a slacker without the gumption to tie his own shoes. Grandma considers that Red's condition, as she puts it, of being an impudent gawk of an apple that did not fall far from the tree, is ultimately attributable to bad blood, Father being but one in a long line of blithering idiots, dried-up hags, and drooling gawms on both sides of his unfortunate family and if truth be told, Red is fortunate that *he's* not a raving lunatic. Yet.

These injunctions occur at irregular intervals, and most usually follow incidents that explosively end in spirited punishment of one sort or another of Red. Grandpa says that he'll be happy to be a father to Red, just lead him to the bar in Pat's Tavern. But he relents, and he and Red take strained walks in the park, or sit in virtual silence at the end of the 69th Street pier and watch the busy shipping in the Narrows, or stand behind the wire-mesh fence and catch an inning or two of a tavern-league softball game. On these outings, Grandpa says very little, although occasionally he says that Red should keep himself clean: when he gets older: for the pure Catholic girl: he'll meet someday: soon. Grandpa adds: sooner than Red thinks, and sighs despairingly.

They sit at the end of the pier on a grey, blustery afternoon, watching a tug shoulder a small tanker into the central channel leading to the open sea. Grandpa lights a Lucky Strike, expertly shielding the match flame from the stiff salt wind, an act that Red suddenly sees as graceful and troublingly uncharacteristic. Grandpa takes a drag and says that Red should keep away from the bad element, especially the bums who are in that terrible class of his at school, he wouldn't be surprised if they all wind up in the electric chair, and thank God the term is not forever. He smokes in silence, neither adding to his remarks nor waiting in expectation of an answer, finishes his cigarette, and flicks the butt into the slow glossy swells that move past them ceaselessly.

Grandpa looks at Red and puts his hand on his shoulder, the touch tentative, nervous, noncommittal. He says that yes, Red will soon be out of that class of moron criminals and before you know it he'll be in high school or he'll be somewhere. He'll be gone. Grandpa puts his hands in his lap. He says that soon Red will be a man. Red looks at Grandpa, there's something odd in his voice, his face is dark and grim and hard, and he looks older and younger at the same time. Grandpa says that Red will have to go somewhere, go away somewhere when the time comes, join the Navy or something, go *away* somewhere. When the time comes, it's only wise. He says that Red has to think about getting away from Grandma, getting the hell away from Grandma! He says that Grandma will suck the life out of him but he still has a chance to be a boy if he.... He still has a chance to be a man, anyway. Maybe. Grandpa says that Grandma is a little crazy and that if he had any moxie *he'd* get away from her but he doesn't have any moxie, he never had any, he knows that Father thinks he's a mollycoddle and by Christ the no-good drunken son of a bitch is right, he *is* a God damn mollycoddle! He says that he might as well be dead. Red is terrified at what Grandpa is saying and by the papery timbre of his voice, whispery and weak. He's afraid to look at him. He's afraid to touch him. He makes himself look.

Red wants to see. He wants to *see*. Grandpa's face is so bleak that Red feels a chill. Grandpa is ashy white. Grandpa lights another cigarette and says something that Red doesn't hear. Grandpa is smoking and talking and looks terrible.

THIRTY FOUR

❖

Ever since the day on the pier, Red thinks that something is the matter with Grandpa because he speaks of things that Red is pretty certain he's not supposed to know about: Grandpa doesn't seem to care. Over a period of some months, he takes Red aside every few days and tells him something about himself or Grandma or Mother or Father or some other member of the family. These revelations are not in any way prefaced, but stated bluntly as isolate, self-enclosed fragments. Some of this knowledge makes Red uneasy, some disgusts him, some simply puzzles him. By and large, however, as with most unsought-for knowledge, it numbs him in direct proportion to that which it reveals.

Grandma is afraid of cats, hats on the bed, and looking into mirrors. When possible, she poisons every cat she can. Mirrors, of course, have the Devil inside them, and if you look at yourself long enough he will possess your soul. Cats, too, Grandma believes, are hosts for the Devil. Grandma sometimes says that priests are really nuns in the nighttime, and that the few real nuns there are, if there are any at all, spend their time gorging on roast beef and thinking up ways to punish bad children, of whom the world is full. She says that the Church has a plan for all of them, oh yes.

Grandma likes to wear rags.

Grandma's dream books guide much of her life, for she believes in and fears their decisive interpretations. She can often be found sitting up in the middle of the night, a dream book in her lap, sobbing with terror.

Grandma throws salt over her shoulder every morning to keep away the spirits of the dead, which are everywhere, but mostly favor the electric wall outlets: the dead like to enter a living person's house as electric light. That's why spirits are not seen in the daytime.

Niggers can't be priests because they're really animals, like baboons. The Pope is not really an Italian, at least not a riffraff wop spaghetti-bender.

Grandma's souvenirs occupy most of the top drawer in her bureau and she most cherishes the matchbooks and paper napkins taken from saloons, roadhouses, and restaurants. Sometimes, shaking with fear in the middle of the night, she puts all of these particular keepsakes on the top of the bureau in alphabetical order, moaning to herself for God to help her. Sometimes she tells Grandpa a story connected with one of the places from which a napkin or matchbook comes: it is always about some fine figure of a man with a beautiful head of hair on him who couldn't take his eyes off her while Grandpa was up to Christ knows what foolishness with yet another fair-weather friend, knocking back the whiskey at the bar.

Grandma's three fur coats from the year one go into storage every summer and Grandma checks every week to make sure that nobody has stolen them because you can never tell with the kikes who own the fur business.

Grandma lost a child at birth two years after Mother was born, thank God. Another daughter.

Grandma's mother and father, and Red can get down on his knees and thank God that they passed away while he was still a baby, spent their lives in a kitchen lit by one forty-watt bulb, living on oatmeal with oleo, trembling and shaking with the fear of some shanty-Irish God they themselves created. The old man was a member of the K of C and the Holy Name Society and Christ knows what other creeping-Jesus societies and spent all his life on retreats, squirming and gawking in front of doddering priests, and the old lady lived for the Church, with her daily Mass and Benediction and Confession, beJesus the priests must have died of boredom with her telling over what she thought were her sins. The old biddy didn't want Grandma to marry Grandpa, he was what she called hoity-toity, but if truth be told it's because he can take the Church or leave it, the whole shebang is a lot of mumbling and superstition as far as Grandpa is concerned. And Grandma was under that old bitch's thumb all the days of the curse-of-God woman's life, with her sinful this and her sinful that, and the old man with his finger stuck in a missal or a catechism or some God damn pamphlet or other, nodding his pitiful head. It's a wonder with the sins flying around so thick that they were man and wife at all, and Red will understand what Grandpa means soon enough. Too soon enough! Grandpa walked in on Grandma unintentionally one day soon after they were married, and there the poor girl was, beating herself with a belt across her back and her stomach and legs and saying the Our Father and Hail Mary and Apostles' Creed and the Act of Contrition with the tears streaming down her face, beJesus it was enough to melt a heart made of stone. She was fit to be tied, and got as red as a beet, but it was soon clear to Grandpa that she was mortified because Grandpa was looking at her lashing herself in her shift, because she was in her shift. She told Grandpa to stay away from her for she had come to realize that sins of

luxury lead quickest to Hell. Of course, Grandpa still had a little life in him then, although there's room for regret there.

Grandma throws salt over her shoulder to chase away the
bad spirits for sometimes they won't go back into the wall outlets even when the light is turned off. She says that she can
hear them whispering inside the light bulbs.

Grandma says that all priests and some nuns, the old dried-
up ones, can read people's thoughts: she loathes and fears
them and always says that it's too bad that her dear mother
and father didn't know just how terrible priests can be, she's
heard many a story that a good number of them are really
jews, yes, jews in disguise so as to take advantage of good
Catholic women. Grandma struck a nun with a window pole
when she was in the fifth grade, because she saw a red halo or
mist around the nun's head and knew that she was not a nun
at all but some class of demon.

Although she pretends otherwise, Grandma is glad that Red
can't get into parochial school because Mother is a divorced
woman and in a state of perpetual sin. Grandma says that
parochial school is not all that it's cracked up to be and while
it is all right, by and large, for girls, it makes boys into self-
abuser morphodites and sissies who like to put on their mothers' clothes and they stay that way forever.

Grandma's older sister died of consumption, Grandpa says
it was of meanness, soon after he and Grandma were married.
She was a cruel woman, a spinster made out of ice with a heart
as cold as the grave. At her funeral, Grandpa sat with some
distant greenhorn relatives with the smell of peat smoke and
manure still in their clothes while Grandma was with her
mother and father and some kiss-ass old drunk of a priest all
of them drowning in snots and tears and calling on Jesus
Christ to take this beloved child of the Church into His merciful arms. It was enough to make a cat laugh. Grandpa says

that he was worried that the old bat would knock the lid off her coffin to screech about the accommodations. She was a dragon and it's a pity to say so but Grandma has some of her character, so she has.

For instance, Grandma never wished Mother and Father well on their marriage, no, on the contrary, she put a curse on it. Grandpa says that he hates to say so, but she did indeed put a curse on her own flesh and blood, a wish that Mother shouldn't have a day of happiness. But Grandma had no objection to playing up to Father right after the marriage, making him highballs of a Sunday afternoon, dancing with him like some kind of horse's ass of a chippie, a woman her age, in front of Mother and Grandpa, it was what might be called shameless, and making a fool of herself in front of Jimmy Kenny sometimes or some other shiftless leech in the family, saying things about stealing such a handsome man away if Mother didn't watch her step and mind her p's and q's. And after the marriage ran into trouble Father was suddenly some drooling rummy with not a decent bone in his body. Not that Grandpa has a good word to say about a man who has no stomach for his responsibilities, but fair is fair, fair is fair.

Grandpa says that after Red was born, Mother soon put a stop to Grandma's minding him so that she and Father could go out to a movie, or to have a couple of drinks with people their own age, or to have a bite of chop suey in the neighborhood. It's because Grandma took to slapping Red across the face if he cried or soiled himself or jumped up and down in his crib, as babies, for Christ's sake, are bound to do, or did anything but sleep. And they were no love taps either, but beJesus, good healthy swats across Red's little face. Grandpa made it his business to tell Mother about it and never heard the end of it. Even to this day, he hears the lectures on a husband's duty and loyalty. That strikes Grandpa funny and he says that he hasn't been a husband to Grandma for years, nor she a wife to him. Grandma said that she ought to have whaled Mother when *she* was a baby rather than let her walk all over her, maybe she'd have stayed at the good cashier's job in Trunz's pork store instead of growing up to be some flighty chippie running around to Rye Beach and Bear Mountain and Coney Island and every other God damn place with the neighborhood trash, guineas and polacks, bad actors who weren't even Catholic, some of them. But they liked their booze, and the girls with their skirts that showed everything were no worse than Mother.

Grandma always said that she worshiped the ground her mother and father walked on, but it was more like fear than worship if you ask Grandpa, the two old religious fanatics got to the point where they didn't believe their confessors were real priests for the little penances they gave them, but what in the name of God Almighty did the two of them ever do? They were barely alive! So the old lady took to licking the church floor, crawling on her hands and knees up the aisle to the altar rail, thumping her craw and moaning, and the old man would do things like hold in his water and his bowels until he rolled on the floor in agony, they were no better than holy rollers, pathetic to see them. It was God's blessing that they were taken when they were, for whatever God may be, it's sure that He can't stand to see such ugliness.

For some years after the two of them passed away, Grandma would hide under a table or in the bathroom or in the closet if a bird landed on the window ledge, but to this day Grandpa has no idea why. She also tormented herself after Confession that she hadn't confessed all her sins, or told how many times she sinned, or how serious they were, or how many times she thought about committing them, and on and on, it was criminal to listen to her hour after hour. She thought that she'd be struck dead at the altar rail or that her tongue would swell up all black in her mouth like a balloon at the touch of the Host. Finally, the Host made her sick to her stomach just to think about it and she said that God was giving her a message by making her sick as a dog, it was the same thing as the dirty birds that landed on the window ledge whenever they felt like it, by Christ Grandpa couldn't make head or tail out of what she said, but she stopped going to Mass and God forgive him but it was a load off his mind.

Grandpa says that the first Christmas that Mother and Father celebrated in their new apartment, neat as a pin it was, Grandma gave them a pound of navy beans for a present, it's the God's honest truth. Grandpa was ashamed to be a party to it but Grandma has ways, she has ways. Mother was cut to the quick, mortified, really, but Father made a great thing out of it and joked that more people should think of the practical side of Christmas, navy beans were just the ticket, and he said that he was pretty sure that the Wise Men brought navy beans to the infant Jesus in his manger, no matter what the priests say. Grandma almost exploded to hear her meanness made a joke out of, and she ranted and raved that God in His wisdom would see to it that such blasphemy landed Father in Hell. She got even when he was out of work and Mother was carrying Red when she told them that they'd have to go to Sister Elizabeth's Lying-In Hospital clinic, a God damn butcher shop, did Mother and Father think that she was made of money? Grandpa says that he was ashamed, but Grandma, well, Grandma. She held the purse strings as she still does.

Grandma gave cousin Katy a ratty boa all bare patches where the skin showed through, not fit for a nigger to wear, it was a terrible piece of rubbish that her mother had left her, and that should have been buried with her to spare the rest of us the sight of it, and Grandma to this very day speaks of

Katy's ingratitude for the wonderful fur, it's enough to make anybody die laughing.

As time went on, Grandma started to get worse and worse about things, she wouldn't spend 2¢ on the *Daily News,* and when she tried to make Grandpa choose between a pack of butts every two days and his lunch, he's ashamed to say that he cried like a child until she relented and told him that he could eat lunch too, and then she lectured Mother on how Grandpa worked like a slave.

Slave is the word to use for the way Grandma took to looking; and Grandpa says that he has asked her time and again until he is blue in the face to wear something other than the tatters and rags that she wears around the house, the shreds and patches and all of it unraveling into flitters, there's no reason for her to make a spectacle of herself. Grandma sneers and says that she's sorry that she can't measure up to the bitches and sluts in Grandpa's office stinking of five-and-ten perfume in their short skirts and their silk stockings, she's a respectable married woman with a cross to bear and she'll never stoop to looking like some cheap floozie.

Grandpa says that she staggers into the bedroom every night, drunk on beer, then falls onto the bed and tells him that her life is such an ordeal that she can't wait to be at peace in her grave and away from all of them, by Jesus Christ's Blessed Mother, she's a saint on earth to put up with the ordeal her life is, what with him and Mother and that snotfaced Red, the insolent pig of a child, she is a saint!

Grandpa says that he's got a suit that he bought six years ago that she's never let him wear. He hasn't an ounce of courage, and many a time he's thought that, but Grandma has ways.

Grandpa says that the last time he went over to Jersey to visit Katy she took him in the bathroom and showed him the scars that Grandma's beatings with hangers and belts and a switch left on her back and shoulders and arms and thighs. Grandpa says that he cried, merciful Christ, he cried like a baby.

Grandpa cries. To Red's contempt.

THIRTY FIVE

❖

Grandma's terrible voice, in high-pitched attack upon somebody who has or had the temerity to be alive, is fading into darkness and oblivion as Red edges into sleep. Images crystallize, fade, are reconstituted, Grandma and Grandpa at their shifting centers, in curious scenarios. Suppose that Grandpa,

in rakishly angled straw boater, should accidentally push Grandma headfirst into a deep tray of Mr. Dreyer's potato salad:

in crisp ice-cream suit should insouciantly seal her in the cellar with her photographs forever:

in white high-collared shirt should take her to Canarsie and haphazardly leave her in a vacant lot:

wearing a dark tie and small stickpin, should inadvertently lock her in a room with twenty priests:

mandolin shining under his arm, should randomly push her off the roof:

in dark-grey pin-striped suit, should aimlessly order her to go out barefoot for beer every night:

in faded khaki pants, should casually place her in cold storage with her ratty fur coats:

navy-blue scarf about his neck, should incidentally sell her
to the ragman for a quarter:

pitcher of beer clutched in one hand, should blithely hang
her with one of her leather belts:

smoking a Lucky Strike, should breezily choke her with a
dozen charlotte russes:

squinting through rimless pince-nez, should frivolously
decide that she be made chief cook and bottlewasher for
Jimmy Kenny and his floozie:

drunk on Wilson's "That's All" should nonchalantly put her
on a subway to the remotest Bronx:

after winning every hand at Casino, should offhandedly
smack her in the face with a cold head cheese:

with dark hair and jaunty pipe, should coldly use her as col-
lateral to back up his bets with a bookmaker:

along with Alex, his late brother, should carelessly misplace
her in the Savage Wilds of the Dark Congo:

adorned with emerald-green Erin Go Bragh lapel ribbon,
should debonairly dump a pail of ravenous lice on her head:

in grey Homburg, should glibly force her to attend open
school in her household tatters:

smiling with dazzling false teeth, should aloofly make her
receive Communion until she pukes her guts up in church:

in highly polished black shoes and black silk socks, should
serenely give her the clap-siff and then send her to Kings
County clinic with the greaseballs and hunkies:

toying with his sterling silver penknife, should smoothly put
runs in the twenty-three pairs of silk stockings she's never
worn:

the scorecard of Dazzy Vance's 1925 no-hitter against

Philadelphia in one hand, should suavely knock out her gold tooth with a claw hammer:

moist-eyed over his father's cigar cutter, should buoyantly knock out her brownish-black tooth with a perfectly thrown gold brick:

after consulting his heirloom pocket watch, should cheerfully make her attend Katy's cripple of a husband all day long, seven days a week:

reserved in his black-and-white spectators, should gaily arrange for her to make supper for and eat with the Rongo brothers every evening:

musing over a dried gardenia pressed in the pages of *Modern Business English*, should jauntily force her to Confession, in the rectory, with a convert priest:

a photograph of Mae Marsh in *Intolerance* held to his heart, should joyfully volunteer her services for perpetual charity work with the Sisters of Mercy:

looking up from his graceful, fragile handwriting, should merrily find her a job cleaning toilets in a Bowery flophouse:

his grey hair gleaming with lilac-scented pomade, should desultorily sell off her jewelry to buy gifts for the bimbo slut tramps at the office:

his face thickly lathered with Barbasol, should calmly drop an anvil on her feet:

contemplating his Gem nail clipper, should easily torment her into buying butter rather than oleo:

in his velvet-collared Chesterfield, should effortlessly pitch her false teeth out the window:

with his mother-of-pearl opera glasses about his neck, should gracefully forget her in Phil the butcher's freezer:

rattling his tin can full of pencil stubs from work, should impassively deny her the pretzels she covets:

pulling on his grey suede gloves, should tell her, insouciantly, that he is going out on the town with Father:

And suppose that Grandpa, in rented morning clothes, a perfect boutonniere in his buttonhole, should decisively have left Grandma waiting at the altar some thirty-five years ago?

THIRTY SIX

❖

Red is suddenly and inexplicably sexually infatuated with Patsy Taylor, a small blond girl with a pinched, worried look on her pallid face. Patsy is about Red's age, goes to Catholic school, and lives in a building three doors down from Red's. How is it, then, that he just now notices the way she jumps rope and plays potsy and jacks? How is it that he just now becomes aware of the way her plaid uniform skirt flies up on her legs when she runs?

Where has she been?

Red's infatuation daily grows greater, until he is virtually crazed with lust. Patsy, Patsy. How beautiful are her protruding front teeth! Stay Red with flagons, comfort him with apples.

One evening, Red pretends to catch up, accidentally, with Patsy as she is going in to supper. He says that he thinks he knows her from school, yeah. He thinks so. He says that he thinks they might have been in the same class when they were little, that maybe they were eraser monitors once? In the same class? He lies fervently, trying not to look at the tiny breasts that swell her white, ink-spotted blouse. Maybe they were blackboard monitors? Patsy looks at him with perfectly cruel grey eyes and says that she hears that Red is one of the kids in the feeb class. She says that they don't have any feeb kids in Catholic school, and that she's never been in any class with Red because she's always gone to Catholic school. She says that girls don't have to clap erasers in Catholic school, that's for the boys to do. Red says that the class he's in does not mean a thing, not a thing, it's a mistake. Patsy gives him a cold sly grin, her little rabbit mouth partly open. Red feels humiliation enveloping him and abruptly veers away from this school talk to ask her (temptress Patsy! shining Patsy!) crudely, stupidly, if she'd like to have a present? Some presents? Can he maybe give her? Maybe a? Maybe some? Patsy smiles at him again and touches his hand with one dirty finger. Red looks stupidly at her pale face. Patsy touches his hand with two dirty fingers, then turns and runs up the stoop into her building. Red smells his hand. Oh, Patsy! Oh, Patsy does want a present! Red starts home, his heart thick in his chest.

Presents? But Red has no money.

Three days pass, a week passes. Patsy's vague bucktoothed smile for Red wavers, then fades, and finally disappears. She says that she didn't really expect a moron feeb to even know what a present is! She is throwing a filthy, bald tennis ball up into the air over and over again and catching it with awkward stiff fingers. It stabs Red's heart. It makes him want to kiss her shoes. It makes him want to cry.

And then Grandma tells Red to go to Dreyer's for a dime's worth of the medium butter, not the best butter, the *medium butter*, and tell the nazi kraut, if he's still ignorant of the fact after all these years, whose grandson Red is, because if Grandma gets one iota less than she's paying good American money for to some heinie who, if truth be told, is probably sending it over to Hitler or whatever the damn fool's name is, she'll see to it that Red learns how to run an errand! Red nods and assumes his patient, mistreated-dog look, another disguise in a rapidly growing repertory. The dime for butter is Patsy's dime, Patsy's.

The butter does not exist, nor does Grandma, anywhere on earth.

Patsy is playing jacks on her stoop and Red waves to her. She stares at him insolently. Oh how desirable is the homely Patsy in her fine disdain.

The butter dime is as good as spent, the butter can go screw itself, and Grandma can go straight to Hell. In a delirium of passion, Red buys a nickel ring on which is depicted a garish, gruesome representation of the Sacred Heart, girdled with thorns and dripping blood, the image protected by a layer of celluloid, a four-cent top painted bright green, and a penny's worth of red-hot dollars. He asks for these things to be put into a paper bag, and then he runs back to wonderful Patsy's wonderful stoop so as to place his offerings in her wonderful dirty hands. Patsy looks into the bag, smiles her rodent smile, and gets up. She gathers up her jacks and ball and beckons for Red to follow her into the building, along the ground-floor corridor, and into the gloomy little space beneath the stairs, next to the door that leads out to the courtyard.

Patsy is talking about something, the Sacred Heart or the Infant Jesus of Prague or Mother Superior or the tormented souls in Purgatory for fifty million years of terrible suffering. She gives Red some candy, she puts the ring on her little finger, she says that she thinks it's beautiful. She says that she loves the top, too, she just loves green, it's just her favorite color. Red is grinning foolishly, trying to hide his stained teeth with his hand. He laughs uncontrollably, then leans over and kisses

Patsy on the cheek. Patsy blushes, Red blushes, then Patsy leans over and kisses Red on the mouth and he thinks, for a moment, that his entire face is going to burst into flames. There is a dull, thrilling ache in his groin.

Patsy chews a red-hot dollar with her funny little mouth, her face pink and sweaty. She shifts so as to sit cross-legged and Red can see up her skirt to the crotch of her white under-pants. With the tingling after-sensation of her mouth on his mouth and the partial display of her underwear, Red gets an erection that is suddenly so stiff that it hurts. He is afraid that Patsy can see the bulge it makes in his threadbare corduroy knickers and hunches over to hide his lap from her.

Feverish, joyous, ecstatic, embarrassed, and grateful to Patsy, beautiful open-thighed Patsy, Red accepts another red-hot dollar. Oh dirty, careless Patsy! Can it be that she is open-ing her legs a little more, can it be that her skirt has ridden up a little higher? He can see more of her. Or something. Some-thing. He knows that he is leering like some morphodite, like Sal Rongo or Whitey, his head is swimming and light. Patsy says that she has to go in to supper and she kisses him again, sugary-cinnamon sticky, her hand accidentally brushing against his terrible and shameful lump. She says thanks, or she says thank you, or she says thank you Red. *Red*, she says *Red*. Her little front teeth catch her thin lower lip.

When Red gets home, his pathetically ridiculous story about the lost butter dime fairly well formed in his mind, Grandma tells him, before he can say one lying word, that it's not bad enough that he should be a cheat and a loafer and a God damned liar and a bulletheaded moron, oh no, but that, Jesus Mary and Joseph, now he's a sneak thief as well! She lashes him with the buckle end of her belt and Red screams despite himself. Grandma says that by Jesus he's to stay away from that scrawny little consumptive slut down the street with the teeth in her face like a sewer rat and a chin that could slice cheese, or she'll cut his legs out from under him, by Christ she will! She lashes Red again and breaks the skin on his back as he half-turns away, then belts him five or six more times. Then he's sent out for the butter. When he returns, she hits him again. He's bleeding slightly from the broken welts on his back, sides, legs, and buttocks, and Grandma tells him to go and wash himself and put some iodine on his scratches and get to bed without any supper. Mother is crying and she says that Red must really stay away from that little tramp, and that she didn't raise him to steal. Red looks at her with fierce contempt. The bitch.

In bed, his body sore and stinging, Red thinks about Patsy, about her legs and her mouth and her shameful underpants and her crotch. Her little hidden pussy. He begins to abuse himself, to defile himself, to make Patsy do dirty and filthy things to the pure temple of his body, that temple given to him by a loving God. Well, fuck it! Oh Patsy, oh Patsy, dirty darling dear, open your legs and let me see you, you little tramp.

THIRTY SEVEN

❖

Red and Patsy sit on the ground in the dim quiet of the dense bushes that border a rarely used footpath in the park. Red says that he feels really lousy that Patsy got spanked for what happened a few days ago, and he got spanked, too, well, *he* got whipped, she can see for herself if she wants, the bruises. He eyes Patsy nonchalantly and says that he doesn't really care, he says that he doesn't give a *shit* about being whipped! He's used to being whipped, being whipped is old stuff to Red, he laughs it off.

Can he somehow, he wonders, get Patsy to sit with her legs open again?

Patsy says that she's kind of a little afraid to be here with Red because if whoever saw them last time sees them again, Patsy says she'll get killed, she'll just get killed. She looks again at Red, her mouth, half-open, working juicily at two pieces of Fleers Dubbl-Bubbl Gum. She says that it was probably Red who got them in trouble because he talked so loud that day the way he talks loud a lot from being, probably, in the idiots and morons class all day long.

Red looks at her mouth and her dirty, scabbed-over knees. He thinks of her sticky kisses, her hand accidentally touching him, *maybe* it was accidental. He wants to put his hands on her, inside her blouse, up her skirt, into her underpants. Her worn plaid skirt is at mid-thigh. Red asks if she likes the gum, and Patsy nods, chewing. Red hasn't told her he almost got caught stealing it from that new kike candy-store guy, the rat. Patsy pouts a little and says that she thought that maybe he'd buy her another top or a Duncan yo-yo, or maybe some new jacks, the kind that are all different colors. She says she wouldn't have come to the park with him and into the bushes just for some bubble gum. Red says that he'll have something really neat for her next time and Patsy says that she won't talk to him any next time, she's scared to death, she must be nuts to be here now. Red laughs and says that he bets that Patsy's father gives her a couple of love taps on her rear end and she screams bloody murder. She ought to see what his Grandma uses to beat the God damn shit out of him. Patsy makes a face and says that it's a sin to use bad language like that all the time. Red ignores her and says that he's used to being whipped and he doesn't care anymore even though he did care when he was little. Red looks at her little breasts, and says that, besides, he's got a secret word to keep anything, anything at all, from hurting him. He leans back into the shadows on one elbow and looks up Patsy's skirt.

Patsy asks him what he's talking about. She asks him what secret word he knows, she says that there's no such thing as a secret word, she asks him what the word is. Red's penis is stiff and he wonders what Patsy would do if he just pulled it right out of his pants. He smiles, carefully keeping his hated teeth covered with his upper lip. He says that the special word can keep anybody who says it from feeling anything, smacks or wallops or punches, he swears to God. He says that, for instance, Patsy's father could pull her underpants down and spank her bare behind with his hand or a belt or a brush and she wouldn't feel a thing. Red flushes with the thought of Patsy's bare behind stuck out and her underpants down around her knees. Oh Jesus Patsy, Christ Patsy, you tramp.

Patsy starts to giggle uncertainly but her eyes are focused unwaveringly on Red's face. Red says distractedly that he wonders if Patsy follows the Dodgers because his Father once bumped into Dolph Camilli in Ebinger's buying a box of butter cookies, really, butter cookies! Red looks up through the screen of leaves at a slice of the grey sky. Patsy's behind, bare. Pins and needles are tingling in Red's crotch, but it feels numb, too. Patsy asks what the secret word is, she says that she wants to know but she doesn't believe it, but she'll give him a kiss if he tells her. Her incisors are glistening with spit and Red is looking straight up dirty Patsy's Our Lady of Angels skirt and he feels like tearing it off her. He feels like he'd like to shoot his scum all over her scuffed, old, play shoes. He says that he can't tell her, his voice shaking so much that it sounds as if somebody is inside him talking through his mouth. Patsy says he can tell her, he *can*, he's mean if he won't, and that if she knew a magic word even though she knows there's no such thing as a magic word, she'd tell *him*.

Red leans back on both elbows, he doesn't care if Patsy sees that he's got a boner, he even sort of wants her to see that he has, he feels as if he's going to go crazy. He looks at her wet, busy mouth, and says that he'll tell her but she has to promise to let him touch her anywhere he wants if he does. Patsy says she has to let him touch her? Touch her where? Red says that he told her, for Pete's sake, she has to let him touch her anywhere he wants to touch her. Patsy chews her gum very fast and says that that's fine, go ahead and tell her, she promises to let Red touch her like he says if he tells her. Red says that the magic word is greentop. Patsy looks at him and sneers, she says she wants the real word, what the heck is greentop? Red says he swears to God and hopes to die if it's not the real word. Patsy grins archly and says that he just bought her a green top the other day, a *green top*. Red sits up and says so what! He says that's one of the reasons he bought the God damn top, that maybe her just having it would bring her luck. She looks at him doubtfully and he says that he swears to God Almighty and may he be struck dead right here on the spot if that's not really really the secret word. He says that Patsy just has to say the word to herself three times, sort of under her breath, just before she's going to get spanked and she won't feel anything. He crosses his heart and says that he really hopes to die if he's lying. Patsy is uncomfortable but impressed by the blank staring sincerity of Red's dull face, beet red and slick with oily sweat. He says well, so? Patsy closes her eyes and tucks her blouse in nervously and nods yes. Red moves closer to her in the gloom gathering amid the thick-leaved branches. He says that it'll be fine, she'll like it, then clumsily and brutally pushes her skirt up to her skinny hips and puts his hand between her legs. Patsy catches her breath and opens her eyes wide with fright.

Red isn't sure how any of this is happening and he doesn't care, either. Patsy is crying very softly because Red says that if anybody sees them they can put them away in reform school or even the crazy house, especially girls because they figure that girls who do this stuff are just born hooers especially if they're only eleven or twelve. He says that they won't blame *him* because they know he's in the stupid class at school and they expect him to be a moron and he'll tell them anyway that

Patsy talked him into it and even unbuttoned his fly and who the hell will believe some dopey story about a magic word for God's sake. His erect penis is out of his knickers and he's forced Patsy's hand onto it, Jesus Jesus! Red doesn't give a damn about anything, especially Patsy, who is just her hand moving up and down on him as he shows her how. She disgusts him with her face ugly with fear and her buck teeth stuck out of her mouth that's circled by a ring of sticky dirt and the tears running down her cheeks, God what a hooer she is! Red reaches down and clutches at, then pulls her underpants down and then off and throws himself on top of her. He has no idea exactly what to do but he knows he's supposed to get into her, he shoves his erection into the space between her legs, blindly thrusting, then he feels himself inside her, a little. Patsy sobs and bites her knuckles with her ugly rat teeth and Red pushes as hard as he can but she's too small or too tight or something but it doesn't matter because at his second shove he begins to shoot his load, oh wow Jesus God! all over her belly and thighs and he spurts on her skirt and every other place, he can't control, he can't help what he's, he's just rubbing it anywhere and coming all over the place, sweet Jesus!

It's almost dark. Red and Patsy walk silently through the park back to their block. Patsy's skirt is a little damp where she washed off the scum stains with water from a drinking fountain. She's crying louder now and Red looks at her, disgusted, she can kill herself crying for all he cares now, they're just walking along, but he's a little worried. He says that she better go ahead because they don't want anybody to see them and shoot off their big mouth. He stands very close to Patsy and holds her arm at the elbow and says that she better not tell anybody what happened or else he'll say that he saw her pull her underpants down to show Bubbsy and Kicky and all the other guys her pussy down in the cellar and that she let Big

Mickey fuck her, right, and that's why they sent him back to reform school. Red says that he'll lie until he's blue in the face and even if they don't believe him and even if he gets thrown out of school and beaten to within an inch of his life, he doesn't care because in a few years he'll join the Marines. Red says that he bets *she* cares if she gets expelled because that will be the end of Bishop Molloy or Fontbonne Hall, where they don't allow little sluts. Patsy nods her head, the tears rolling down her pale, dirt-streaked face, and turns to go. Red watches her walk away in the dusk, her thin shoulders slumped, Jesus, what a scarecrow.

Red leans against a lamppost and realizes that he feels terrific, he feels wonderful.

Red feels like some guy in a dirty book. With Blondie or Ella Cinders.

Red feels like a man.

Red feels like busting Sal Rongo in the face just for laughs, he feels neat, neat.

Red thinks of Patsy, that tramp, what a pushover, and her crap, making believe she didn't want to do it, all snots and tears. Jesus, the little slut.

Red starts to laugh out loud. He thinks that it will give the little crybaby something to fucking knock the priest flat with in Confession, she'll have to say Hail Marys for a hundred years and crawl up the aisle of the church on her hands and knees like the old guinea ladies in their black dresses.

THIRTY EIGHT

❖

The Filipino champion will be outside Woolworth's at four o'clock, *HIS ONLY NEIGHBORHOOD APPEARANCE*, as the poster proclaims. He will perform *TOURNAMENT LEVEL* tricks, not only with the twenty-five-cent Duncan tournament yo-yo but with the ten-cent metal whistler. Duncan has two new tournament colors this year, bright yellow with a black stripe and pale lavender with a white stripe, the latter aimed at girls.

The Filipino!

can do anything,

walk the dog, train in the tunnel, around the world, bower of bliss, rock the cradle, dive bomber, spaghetti, sweet chariot, mashed potatoes, keg of beer, sleeping beauty, the comet, spiderweb, rollercoaster, cat's cradle, swimming pool, and each year, he also demonstrates a newly invented trick, upon which everyone knows that he has worked—day and night—all year long. That's how the Filipino does. He can do all these tricks perfectly, casually, and occasionally will use two yo-yos and perform a different trick with either hand. He stands in the raw grey cold of late spring afternoons, for a half-hour, surrounded by mesmerized children, after which he deftly and swiftly carves into any newly purchased tournament yo-yo, on request, the purchaser's name in a remarkably delicate script. Then he disappears until the following spring.

Red is home by three-thirty, ready to dump his books, change, and run the nine blocks to Woolworth's, so as to be in the presence of a mastery foreign and unattainable, so as to step outside the stupidity that bounds his life, that is his life. He is careful not to reveal to Grandma his overwhelming desire to be gone. For if Grandma were to suspect. He clamps his jaw until it hurts.

Grandma peers at Red as he puts his books on top of the icebox. He avoids her eyes and turns to walk out of the kitchen, pulling off his jacket. She holds up her hand to stop him.

That famous cloud no bigger than a hand appears on the horizon, dark-centered, slow-moving, no bigger than the hand of a woman or a child.

Grandma asks Red where he thinks he's going in such a hurry, she never sees him rush like this when she asks him to bestir himself to help out around the house to show a little gratitude for the roof over his head, but then he doesn't give a shite whether she kills herself keeping the place presentable, he hasn't an ounce of respect, but how could he have any, after all, with the polluted blood that's in his veins? Red says that he's not in any hurry, he's just changing clothes the way he changes clothes after school every day. Every single day. Grandma says that she wants none of his sarcastic lip or she'll knock the snot out of him.

The cloud is a little larger, a little darker.

Grandma follows Red out of the kitchen and into the dining

room, where he drapes his jacket over a chair and starts to unbutton his shirt. She looks at him closely, her eyes narrow and blankly hostile. Red knows that her uncannily suspicious nature is aroused and he lets his jaw hang slack in imitation of Sal Rongo. Grandma says that he certainly looks to *her* as if he's in one hell of a rush, and she wonders why. Then she frowns as he prepares to strip off his shirt, and says that there is no need to change his school shirt today, since his flannel play shirt is dirty, filthy, not fit to be worn by an Armenian, for his Mother, the prima donna, didn't see fit to do the laundry today, out looking, so she says, for a job, although only Jesus Christ Himself knows why, for Grandma can't think for a minute of anybody who'd want to hire a middle-aged woman disgraced by divorce and with a swelled head to beat the band and stuck on herself into the bargain, burdened as she is with a useless lump of a son, a cur of a boy who hasn't even the decency to tell his own grandmother where he's in such a God damned rush to get to! She repins her housedress with the safety pin at her neck and says that it doesn't matter anyway, there's nowhere Red can go now except for right in front of the house, what with him having to keep his good school shirt on. She says that she'll be a monkey's uncle if she lets him wreck and ruin and tear to tatters every decent stitch of clothes he owns, falling and rolling as he does in the gutter like some greenhorn off the boat with the filthy mongrels he thinks are his friends like Big Mikey or Big Kicky, is his name? Whatever the hoodlum's name is he's a bad egg and well on the road to Hell, it's a pity he was ever put on the face of the earth.

Now the cloud begins to cover the sun.

The time is 3:35, and Mother enters the apartment. She's smiling and girlishly excited, and sweating a little. Her face is pretty with lipstick and rouge and she is wearing high heels

and a tan belted polo coat, her best coat. All these things fill
Grandma with bile. Mother says that there's a chance she
might get a job as a waitress at a new coffee shop that's open-
ing just a block away on the corner, the Savory. She'll know
for sure next week. Pleased, she opens her coat to reveal her
navy woollen pleated skirt and white silk blouse.

Red, his shirt half-unbuttoned, watches Grandma turn, glaring, at Mother. Helplessly, he conjures the image of a savage
hound tearing Grandma's guts out through her pussy. Through
her cunt! Oh Jesus. Oh Jesus. Oh Jesus.

Grandma smiles her mocking smile at Mother and says that
it will be a cold day in Hell before they hire her what with all
the little high-school chippies who'll work for next to nothing,
and if by some miracle she gets the job will she be able to hold
her head up in the neighborhood wearing those skimpy uni-
forms that anybody can see right through, they're a disgrace,
they're for sluts and how will she hold her head up? Grandma
makes a face and says that the only reason if truth be told that
they even gave her the time of day is because she's dressed herself up like a chippie herself, that's all those greasy dirty
Greeks want in their filthy greasy spoons.

Tear out her asshole! Dripping fangs. Slavering jaws. Blood.
It's 3:40 the cloud is pitch black and moving faster.

Mother flushes, and pulls her coat around herself, surprised
at the suddenness of this assault. Red is transfixed, his mouth
open. The bitterness of Mother's trapped life overwhelms her,
so that she actually gasps. She turns to Red, gallantly pretending, although her face is red with humiliation, that Grandma
has not spoken. She says that she thought that Red wanted to
go up to the five-and-ten today to see the Duncan Filipino and
it's late?

The cloud balloons into a vast bank of hellish turbulence.
Grandma's eyes light up brilliantly, quite, in fact, beautifully.

They sparkle. Red can hear the deep growls of the hound, gore thick around his muzzle, as he chews Grandma in half, right up the middle.

Grandma says that Red will not be going up to any five-and-ten with his good school shirt on to see any God damn chinaman! She says that Mother can take the blame for not doing the laundry for her own flesh and blood or for that matter for not doing a bit of shopping or cleaning today, instead running around like some damn fool acting half her age with a silk blouse on, she must think that she's some kind of a five hundred dollar millionaire, and wanting to be a waitress! For the love of God in His agony, a waitress, showing herself off to the filthy-minded slobs and hoodlums, the bookies and cab drivers who have nothing better to do than spend their lives drinking coffee on the corner, by the living Christ she has half a mind to report her to the child-cruelty board or whatever it is. Grandma says that Red will not go *anywhere*, let alone the five-and-ten, to Mr. Duncan chink or whoever he may be, probably some maniac of a morphodite hanging around children, by God he'll not go, his flannel shirt is filthy, filthy, and he'll not ruin one of the only decent shirts he has left, the destructive little bastard of an ungrateful child who ruins everything he touches.

In a fit of madness and rage, Red grasps his shirt up near the collar and tears it, raggedly, almost down to its hem. Grandma and Mother stare at him, the high singing of the ripping fabric an echo in the air. Red is crying wildly, blubbering that the God damn school shirt is no God damn good any God damn more and he doesn't give a good God damn!

Grandma steps up to him and hits him across the face so that blood, snots, and tears fly, spattering Mother's blouse and skirt: she claws at her lace collar, trying to get her breath.

The cloud covers the entire sky. Red calls out silently, through the pain in his mouth, for the great hound to appear.

Let magic be done. Let Satan produce the beast.

Grandma rubs her hand. She feels put upon by this gawm of a boy and his Mother with the chest stuck out on her like some common tramp in Flynn's saloon. She pulls her hand back again, her face almost serene as small plans creak, snap, founder, and go, wonderfully, under. Life can, indeed, be reasonably satisfactory if not sweet.

THIRTY NINE

❖

Grandma looks up from the soggy newspaper and asks Red where he's going, all dressed up to beat the band, with his good scarf on and his shoes shined. Red says that he's going to take a walk. With Grandpa.

Grandma looks as if she's going to throw up. Her upper lip curls, her lower lip protrudes stiffly, and her eyes goggle. Or maybe she's going to have what they call a fatal stroke.

A *fatal stroke*! You faint and you never wake up from the unconscious coma.

Grandma says, after swallowing the richly putrefacted vomit that surely must be lodged at the base of her throat, that Red has got another think coming if he thinks he's going out of *this* house, no, he'll stay *in* the house, she is God damn sick and tired of him coming and going as he damn well pleases, like some cock of the walk, a twelve-year-old boy! Who still hasn't got his first pair of long pants! He'll stay in, *because*, he'll stay in.

Red says that that's fine with him, he'll stay in. He pulls off his scarf and earflapped lumberjack cap. He knows that his complaisance has saved him the pains of the belt or fist, ring hand or ladle, potato masher or cooking spoon, frying pan or wire hanger, or, God knows, maybe all of them in some arcane order known only to Grandma. She seems especially irritable and nasty today, and Pulciver says that when ladies are like that they call it that they have a rag on, which is some kind of disgusting thing that happens to them when blood comes out of them, *blood*, instead of babies, right from where they piss from, it makes you sick! Pulciver's eyes blink wildly behind his thick clinic lenses. The idea of Grandma bleeding dismays Red, for somebody will have to pay for it.

Grandpa comes into the living room, adjusting his Homburg and then pulling on his grey suede gloves. He looks at Red and says that he thought he wanted to take a walk, how come he's not dressed, where's his mackinaw? Red says that he does want to take a walk. But he can't take a walk. Grandpa lights a Lucky Strike, takes a long drag, and looks at Red through the blue haze of expelled smoke. He says that he does *not* understand what Red is saying, what does he mean that he wants to take a walk but he can't? Red says that he can't explain it any better. He can't explain it at all. But he can't go. Grandpa shakes his head. He says that he can't figure him out, here he is dying of boredom on a winter's Sunday afternoon but he can't go out even though he wants to go out. Grandpa shakes his head again and says that Red ought to be a boy, be a *boy*. He turns and starts to button his overcoat.

Grandma, who has been in the kitchen during this exchange, listening carefully, enters the dining room, making small compassionate noises with pouting lips. She pulls Red against the bosom of her housedress, which smells of fish, grease, and onions, and runs her hand through his hair, taking care to push her fingernails into his scalp and the nape of his neck. She says that Grandpa ought to be ashamed of himself, trying to force the boy out into the gloom and cold and it looks like snow too, when all that Red wants to do is stay home and spend a quiet afternoon chatting with his Grandma, it's been a long time since the two of them had a chat, with the house never still for a moment, if it's not Grandpa bellyaching about the office it's Mother feeling sorry for herself that she hasn't got the gumption to stand on her own two feet, didn't Grandma even have to give her a quarter to go to a movie today!

She gives the lobe of Red's ear a ferocious pinch and Red smiles as tears instantly come to his eyes. Grandma says to Grandpa that he can see for himself if he's not too thick that the poor child can't help but cry—look at him—at being bullied by Grandpa, may Christ have mercy. Grandpa looks at Grandma and then at Red and without a word turns and walks down the hallway to the door.

Grandma says, in a loud, bizarrely false voice that *she'll* not make Red do what he doesn't want to do, the *idea*, trying to force a boy who is as prone to colds and all manner of coughing fits as Red is, to go *out*, the very idea!

The door closes. Grandma gives Red a light rabbit punch, her mouth distorted in what may be a smile.

Red wonders if he were to drop dead right now would he be dead enough not to remember anything. But he is pretty certain that he's not going to drop dead. He's not good enough to drop dead.

Everybody can't drop dead, only the lucky ones. The fucking cocksucker son of a bitches.

FORTY

❖

Red might be able to understand Grandma if he ever discovers how she has been obstructed by:

the tawdry, pitiful, and despised Christmas tree that she reluctantly displays on an end table for a twenty-four-hour period beginning at 10 P.M. Christmas Eve;

her rigid, wiglike coiffure, in stiffness analogous to her corset, in color a preternatural henna;

the tension she displays when she fearfully claims that, once again, she hears rats in the walls;

the Chase & Sanborn coffee cans that she fills with bacon fat, none of which may be used for cooking;

the odd, antic, almost macabre poses she assumes in the mirror when she dresses herself in her ratty, patchy fur coat and the black-veiled hat she bought for her mother-in-law's funeral;

the memories that create the sour expression with which she stares at each cardboard coaster in her mysteriously amassed collection;

the spread-legged position she assumes when sitting in the broken Morris chair, thereby revealing, perhaps inadvertently, her apparent disdain for underwear;

the beer with which she washes down her pretzels, the pretzels with which she sharpens her thirst for beer;

the cider vinegar with which she religiously rubs her temples, forehead, and nape, thereby adding considerably to the somewhat exotic effluvium of her person;

the way her eyelids flutter whenever she is in the near vicinity of a priest or nun, or even a Protestant minister, or a man in a dark suit;

the patronizing bewilderment with which she speaks of Grandpa's business life, the condescending scorn with which she speaks of Grandpa's business colleagues, especially the women;

the mysterious quiddity of her housedresses, which, even when new, look faded and greyly soiled;

the dried and cracked leather handbag, filled to bursting with dimes, which she, on occasion and secretively, holds in her arms while she softly hums;

her insistence that those women who are not drudges, hypocrites, and plaster saints, are sluts, tramps, and painted floozies;

the way in which her face immoderately flushes whenever Red's Father is the subject of conversation neither vituperative nor vindictive;

the rage and indignation with which she speaks of cousin Katy as she details past instances of the punishments and beatings justly meted out, by her, to the ingrate;

the discomfiting because false grief she displays over the sudden death of her mother, a woman known to Grandpa as the bald dragon, some ten years earlier;

the faded, sepia-tone photograph of a dark-haired, buxom

young woman of nineteen or so, which she sometimes claims is of her, while at other times she maintains that it is a likeness of an old friend, Agnes Caffrey, now Sister Francis de Sales;

the five pairs of soft, delicate, beautifully made, and never-worn high-button shoes that are preserved in tissue paper in their shoe boxes;

the cedar chest, to which she has the only key, and into which nobody is permitted to look;

her absolute terror of the cellar storage bin, and indeed, of the cellar itself;

the delight she takes in the deaths of prominent people, all of whom were happy to steal the eyes out of a cripple's head;

her ascent into repressed hysteria and her subsequent descent into depressed exhaustion on those days that Mr. Svensen comes by for the rent;

her belief that Italians and Negroes are racially identical, and that both are directly related to and descended from monkeys;

her suggestion, clear if merely implied, that the dead sometimes make known their wishes through the configuration of the tea leaves left in the bottom of a cup.

But Red will not be able to understand Grandma, for her hidden inhibitions are more profound than her revealed inhibitions. Red may see only that which he may see.

FORTY ONE

❖

Red might be able to sympathize with Mother if he ever discovers how she has been damaged by:

the shame she feels for bearing such loathing for Grandma's Christmas tree, whose display, she persists in thinking, shows, despite all, a good heart;

the knowledge that she may ultimately dye her hair a henna red, that she may ultimately entrap herself in a monstrous corset;

the sound, dryly whispering, of rats in the walls;

her daily, ever-stronger urge to throw out the bacon-fat-filled Chase & Sanborn coffee cans, the sight of which, in the cupboard, makes her scalp itch and tingle;

the fact that she no longer likes to look into the mirror at her naked and sinful body;

the sharp memories of what she thinks of as better days, evoked by the recollection of the places from which came Grandma's mysteriously amassed coaster collection;

her embarrassment and tortured inability to tell Grandma that she, that Red, that anybody, can see her private parts when she sits the way she sits, when she neglects to wear what she neglects to wear;

the whiskey sours she permits men to buy her in Pat's, Gallagher's, the Lion's Den, Flynn's, Henry's, Fritz's, Lento's, and Carroll's taverns, saloons, and bars, and the public sexual liberties of language and act she permits them to take with her;

the nausea that comes over her in waves when she is near Grandma in a close, overheated room;

the impossibility of ridding herself completely of the belief that all priests are fat, rich, lazy, stupid, and gluttonous;

the unwanted image, that of Grandpa surrounded by partially undressed young women, that comes to mind when she thinks of him at the office;

the disgust she feels at laundering Grandma's clothes, especially her tattered, unmatched stockings and her uncannily filthy housedresses;

the overwhelming desire to know just how many dollars Grandma has in the dimes that she thinks are safely hidden;

the confused longing to be either a plaster saint in a transparent negligee, or a painted floozie in a nun's habit;

the discomfort she feels when she considers the cordial past relationship between her ex-husband and Grandma, to which only a fool would give a moment's thought, which only a fool would consider suspicious, which only a fool would think odd;

the nights that she weeps to remember the tortures inflicted on cousin Katy, whose image as a skeletal child in braids and a too-large dress is the one that terribly comes to her, unbidden;

the ceaselessly repressed wish that she has for Grandma's sudden death;

the still occasional suspicion that Agnes Caffrey, now Sister Francis de Sales, is her real mother;

the perpetually nascent belief that the five pairs of old-fashioned unworn shoes in their original tissue-paper wrappings belonged to Miss Caffrey;

the rage she feels toward both herself and Grandma for allowing the latter to put two beautiful tweed suits of hers away in the cedar chest, and then for her concurrence in the pretense that they were given away;

the belief that the cellar harbors the sex-fiend rapist who, Grandma says, has his eye on her as a regular tramp;

the guilty joy she experiences when she, now and again, reads, in error, Grandma's name in the obituaries;

her submission to Mr. Svensen's obscenely paternal embraces and the rank whiskey kisses he plants on her cheek;

her shameful and secret sexual curiosity about Italians and Negroes;

the total, absolute credence she gives to Grandma's readings of tea leaves.

But Red will not be able to sympathize with Mother, for her hidden injuries are more profound than her revealed injuries. Red may see only that which he may see.

FORTY TWO

❖

Red might be able to forgive Father if he ever discovers how he has been demeaned by:

Grandma's annual insults anent the blue spruces he beautifully and lovingly decorated each Christmas that he and Mother were married;

the mockery leveled against his balding head by Grandma, Grandpa, and, most terribly, Mother;

the serious expression he assumed as he agreed that he too could plainly hear rats in the walls;

the raging, idiotic quarrel he had with Mother about the foolishness of her saving bacon fat in Chase & Sanborn coffee cans;

his inescapable image in the mirror, that of a wasted, waxy-complexioned, bleary-eyed, trembling drunk;

Grandpa's taunts regarding the saloons, taverns, bars, cafés, hotels, and roadhouses from which came Grandma's mysteriously amassed coaster collection, as establishments that would not permit Father entrance;

the undeniable fact that when Grandma sat in the Morris

chair, in the way that Grandma chose to sit in the Morris chair, he could not help looking, and looking again, at her exposed sex;

his alcoholic binges, which leave him, sometimes in places that are terrifying, sick, shaking, filthy, broke, and often injured;

the unpalatable but ineradicable truth that Grandma's body odor unfailingly aroused his sexual desire, a cause-effect connection that gradually became clear to Mother, often the object of that desire;

the self-loathing he feels for mocking, often blasphemously, his youthful desire to become a priest;

the surprise he felt when, on a visit, for some reason or other, to Grandpa's office, he discovered that Grandpa was respected and esteemed, and that the young woman who worked as his assistant was enthralled by and attracted to him;

Mother's alarmed bewilderment when he asked her, in their third year of marriage, if she would wear a soiled housedress to bed;

his attempt to persuade Mother to steal a handful of the dimes from the handbag she had told him about;

the excitement he felt at thinking of Mother as a plaster saint of a painted floozie in a nun's habit and high heels;

certain past transactions, accidental and otherwise, physical and verbal, between him and Grandma;

the discomfort he feels at the memory of his friendly visits to wonderful cousin Katy's wonderful Jersey City house, where her drunken, crippled, wonderful husband had, always, a large wonderful supply of gin and whiskey on hand;

the spectre of death that terrifies him, that opens his bladder and loosens his bowels, as he slides into alcoholic unconsciousness;

his coarse remark to Mother and Grandma upon seeing a

brown, faded photograph of a young woman, who is now a nun, the remark being in the nature of a vulgar comparison between the size of the young woman's large bosom and the size of the haloes surrounding the heads of Mass-card-depicted saints;

Grandma's assertion that her old-fashioned shoes, treasured, as she maintained, as souvenirs of her idyllic girlhood, were worth more than he will ever earn;

his corroboration, given Grandma for the price of a quart of Kinsey Silver Label, that Mother's beautiful tweed suits were, indeed, given away;

the memory of his never having been permitted to enter the cellar storage bin without Grandpa's accompaniment;

his callous and vulgar remarks, made for Grandma's amusement, on apparently Jewish names in the obituaries;

his mortification at the hands of Mr. Svensen, for whom he did odd jobs that paid him more than a quarter but less than a half-dollar;

his fear of Italians and their stilettos, of Negroes and their razors;

the fright he gave Mother when he told her, falsely, that Grandma saw his early death in the tea leaves.

But Red will not be able to forgive Father, for his hidden humiliations are more profound than his revealed humiliations. Red may see only that which he may see.

FORTY THREE

❖

Red knows that if Grandma were ever to be hurt, for any reason ... that if, by some chance, Grandma should sustain an injury, receive a wound, damage a hand or foot, endure a puncture, abrasion, incision, or laceration ... that should Grandma, through dread and unthinkable misadventure, be caused to bleed or suffer contusions, bruises or welts ... Red doesn't want to think about what would happen to him, who would of needs be the single reason, the unique cause of Grandma's afflictions or injuries.

If Grandma were to sustain an injury while high on some mountain in far-off Everest, Red would be the cause. And upon Grandma's return to the good old USA she would, upon rising from her terrible sickbed of agony, an agony made virtually unendurable by the proximity of guineas, spicks, chinks, and bohunks, and, Grandma says, through a scowl, maybe even a nigger or two, all of them crammed together in the scowegian slaughterhouse they have the gall to call a hospital, she would, most definitely, after gaining her feet, beat Red so hard that his green and crooked teeth would rattle in his slack, soggy mouth and his pale-blue eyes spout blood. She might be injured almost anywhere. Maybe on the ... roof. On a balmy summer night.

Grandma, on the roof, on a really warm night in midsummer, lots of stars, she seems to be all alone ... no. She's not all alone. Mother is there and, yes, Grandpa is there. Red is there, of course. The four of them in the muggy heat, beneath the stars, the lights of the huge gas tanks on the horizon, out toward Coney Island, blinking red and white. If they ever blow up, everybody will be blown to kingdom come. Not just Red. He likes to keep this in mind.

Grandma says that somebody is a horse's ass, that somebody else is the cock of the walk, that somebody else is a greenhorn trying to pass himself off as a real American, and that somebody else is a shameless tramp no matter that she's also some kind of a holy roller Baptist with her Bible under her oxter and the Sunday-school medals all over her coat. The stars shine down, the heat presses upon them.

There's a ... card table for the pitcher of beer, glasses, a bowl of pretzels. A pack of Lucky Strikes. Grandpa says that it's a wise child that knows something or other and that every dog has a day or barks at the moon. There are three chairs, kitchen chairs, Red sits on something else, Red sits on the roof itself, still warm from the sun that ... Mother says that she thinks that the younger boy looks like her but that he also looks like him, the one who ... Grandma says that nobody knows who belongs to anybody in that family of idiots with their sick polluted blood, they're like a pack of inbred mongrels and as far as she's concerned they all ought to be put away in the crazy house. There's an ash tray on the table. Grandpa's face glows pale red for an instant as he draws on his cigarette. He says that ever since himself made detective first grade, nothing can keep them, or at least her, with the chin on her that could slice cheese, God bless the mark, from acting high and mighty with her nose in the air, and Grandma says it's a pitiful thing to see her mother with that rag of a fur coat on her back, by Christ every time it rains every dog and cat in the neighborhood runs up to it to say hello, it's enough to drive a saint to drink to see such a spectacle, there's nothing on God's green earth like a shanty Irish slattern with two nickels to rub together, beJesus it ought to be against the law.

Is Mother smoking? There's a pack of Virginia Rounds corn-tipped cigarettes on the table, there's a ... plate of cheddar cheese, sliced, and a paring knife with a broken grip, the knife could be the knife that, the thing that ... there's a plate of cheddar cheese, sliced, already sliced, probably in the kitchen before the move to the roof. On this warm, humid night. Starry.

Grandma says that Phil the butcher says that somebody wrapped a baby up in the *Daily News* and put it in an ash can and she certainly would *not* put it past her, and she says that somebody else who got in trouble, shows it off to the priest and everybody else as brazen as you please at Mass every Sunday, looking as if butter wouldn't melt in her mouth, she ought to be horsewhipped along with that gawm of an iceman's son who, ah, you know, beJesus he was in the fourth grade until they had to throw him out when he started to shave, another black guinea with an eye out for a clean American girl.

It seems to be getting warmer, warmer and stickier. The fog horns and the distant clanging of the bell buoys in the Narrows are clear on the heavy air. Suddenly, Grandma starts screaming in agony, pressing one hand into the lap of her skirt. Grandpa stops smoking or he lights a cigarette and Mother drags on a cigarette or puts down a slice of cheddar. Neighbors appear, they're ... they've been on the roof the whole time, they're in a bright harsh light, the rest of the sick and wounded, right over there, at the front of the roof that commands a view of the Dime Savings Bank building downtown. Phillips, Svensen, Astrup, Huckle. Finney, Mertis, Caldwell, McGlade. O'Leary and O'Neill. Finke, Sorensen, O'Brien, Marshall, Moore, Smith. Smythe, Thompson, Rydstrom, Walsh, and Daly. They cluster about the card table, drawn by Grandma's screeches and whimperings. It seems that Grandma's hand is injured, that her hand is ... it seems that she's bleeding. Maybe the knife, the cheese knife ... it's a fish hook. A fish hook has sunk itself into her right index finger. *A fish hook!*

Red knows that a fish hook suddenly discovered deep in the flesh of Grandma's finger can be blamed on nobody but Red, the master of the malign unexpected. There is blood on Grandma's face, hands, and dress, and by the light of an unexpectedly produced light bulb attached to an extension cord, also unexpectedly produced, Grandpa and everybody else can see that the barb is sunk deeply into the flesh so that it cannot be pulled out. Grandma sobs and whines and screams and sweats and writhes, her eyes fixed wildly on Red, the black devil of a boy who will not rest until his Grandma is deep in her grave, but she'll put a dying curse on his bullet head. The hook cannot be pushed out either, because of the eye at the end of its shaft. Its steel is tempered and not breakable, and so Grandma's finger must be cut open. Red turns away to look at the hulking gas tanks, smiling despite his fear, his apprehension, despite the fact that buried in Grandma's cries of pain are threats to his well-being, occluded but still decipherable.

Grandpa has the cheese knife in ... he has his silver pen knife in his hand. He slices, he cuts, he saws, he hacks, he flails away in a fine mist of blood shining in the glare of the electric light. Sweat is running down his face as he attacks the finger, and Grandma is leaning back in her chair, her head lolling stupidly on her shoulder, her tongue, covered with bits of pretzel, protruding, her eyes dull with fear and pain. She whines, doglike. Mother holds her other hand and it pleases Red to see that she has a Virginia Rounds in her mouth and that she could look like some movie star who is a nurse in a savage jungle outpost with teak logs in the river by the waterfall and rain typhoons on the grass roof.

The hook drops out, covered with blood, onto Grandma's lap. There are cheers and applause from the neighbors, all of whom, Red suspects, hate Grandma. Grandpa sighs and thanks God, Mother squints through aromatic smoke and tenderly pats Grandma's cheek. Grandma looks at her raw, savaged finger, then looks at Red, the *inventor* of the fish hook! he who made it to find and pierce Grandma's finger, he whose soul is black with sin and damned.

There's some ... peroxide on the table, and some mercurochrome and a box of bandages and adhesive tape and gauze and ... some iodine. All of a sudden there's a bandage on Grandma's finger and she holds the fat white sausage up for the neighbors to see. She smiles exhaustedly. Her eyes find Red, who comes up to her in a daze and says that he can't figure out how the fish hook that he thought he'd use to catch some filet of sole for supper fell out of his pocket, actually it fell from a box of Crackerjacks or maybe Ralston or a loaf of Silvercup or maybe it's the hook he made from ... a ... from a fish-hook kit that he meant to show Grandpa because ... he's really sorry, he's sorry. Red begins to cry, impossibly, fountains of tears gush from his eyes, he waits for the savage blow that will rattle his brains.

Grandma puts her arm around him, she smiles, she says that anybody can see that it was all an accident, that fish hooks can just appear and be stuck into people's fingers on roofs, on warm nights, warm starry nights, even though Red thinks they can't, Red shouldn't be so silly, and Red shouldn't flinch like that, doesn't Red know that Grandma loves him. The neighbors smile and marvel at Grandma's loving patience, they wonder at the warmth she shows Red, a worthless shambling lout of a boy, a known degenerate who is the stupid son of a flittery woman who couldn't hold on to a husband, what if he takes a drink now and then? Grandma's gold tooth is glittering in the starlight, her glass of beer is held high in a toast to her courage, Grandpa's skill, Mother's cigarette and movie-star looks, and Red's hysterical, uncontrollable weeping. Foolish foolish boy to be afraid of his Grandma, anyone would think that she whips him or something, ha ha ha! As she bends her false smile, her horrible castor-oil smile upon him and the neighbors, Red knows that if Grandma should get a fish hook stuck in her finger, or suffer any kind of injury, here at a card table on the roof or on some mountain in Everest, he will ultimately get hit so hard that his rotting teeth will fly out of his mouth, his eyes will gush blood, and his nuts will explode. He cries helplessly, silently, and Grandma says that he is so sweet, such a sweet child to cry so for her, such a sweet child, there there.

FORTY FOUR

❖

Over so many secretive days, dozens of varieties of penny candy, Mission sodas, Mell-O-Rolls, raspberry tarts, egg creams, ice-cream sodas, slabs of Washington pie, all-day suckers, fish and chips, and the smoke from Wings, Twenty Grands, and Old Golds go into Red's mouth. The orgy seems to go on for so long that Red becomes, in turn, nervous, apprehensive, fearful, and filled with dread. The handful of dimes that he grabbed, in a breathless, panting swoon, from Grandma's bulging handbag, cannot, it seems, be exhausted. Jesus only knows how much he stole. Took. Borrowed. How much he stole. From Grandma.

Whenever he honestly allows himself the clarity of realization that he stole money from *Grandma*, he experiences a terror that slides instantly into hatred. Hidden in the brush and the exhausted weeds down by the freight yards or on a roof or the pier, in the lots or the park, in some cellar coal bin, his mouth full of sweets and the acrid taste of cigarettes, Red says out loud that the old bitch can die and rot and go to Hell. It is on such a day, a week or so after the theft, that Red, churning with loathing at the very fact of life, and in the crazed agony of an insincere and pathetic penance, throws away the few dimes he has left. They glitter momentarily in the pale, hateful sunlight as they soar through the air to land amid the weeds and broken glass, tin cans and dog shit in a far corner of the lots. Red says that that's that, that is God damn that and that is *that*.

He lights up his last cigarette, feeling like a punk, and then, faithful to his sense of the sourness of himself in the unyielding iron world, as soon as he finishes smoking, is on his knees among the weeds, rummaging with his red, chapped hands amid the junk and rubble. He finds three of the dimes and puts them in his pocket. He figures it's good money, he figures what the hell, he snarls and spits at something half out of a soggy paper bag, a dead dog or cat, maybe a baby, swarming with delirious flies, and tells it that the old slob can go and take a flying fuck for herself, then he heads for the candy store to buy a couple more loosies. When he gets fucking old enough to join the fucking marines he'll fucking smoke two fucking packs a fucking day or maybe three fucking packs, and fuck everybody!

As Red enters the apartment that evening, he hears the wild screaming of Grandma and Mother, who is also sobbing and gasping for breath. She is standing in front of Grandma, twitching, and clutching idiotically, in uncontrolled spasms, at the neck and waist and sleeves of her cheap cotton dress, the one that Grandma bought her and that makes her look old and homely and defeated, that makes her look like cousin Katy. Red can't possibly stand this, but he puts on the face that he has learned to put on whenever he thinks he might break something, a face that blankly gazes upon Mother as if she is some dumb bitch of a substitute teacher thrown to the 6A-4 animals. But neither Mother nor Grandma knows he is there.

Grandma holds up her old purse and shakes it in Mother's face. She thinks that, she thinks.

She thinks that *Mother*.

Red flattens himself against the wall of the hallway, in the half-dark, next to the gloomy, fearsome picture of a shadowy lake with three strange dead women at its far shore, ghosts in white. Grandma is getting hoarse, her face is a deathly bluish-grey, and she yells directly into Mother's face, stamping her feet in the torn, shapeless slippers she pulled out of the trash, alternately on the floor, again and again, in a maniacal dance. Mother's face is contorted with weeping, swollen red and wet, and ugly. Red thinks he might throw up.

It's not as if Mother is anybody to worry about, shit, she *is* a sort of tramp, like Grandma says, and what the hell does it matter anyway. Red eases himself down the hallway on tip-toes, to the door, then closes it softly on the wild clamor. He climbs the stairs to sit on the roof for a while. He says that as far as he's concerned the lousy bitches can kill each other, he's tired of taking the blame for everything, no wonder his Father took a powder.

FORTY FIVE

❖

Within a short period, Red has two sexual adventures that are simple if not thoroughly banal. Their major narratives, so to speak, are made of such common stuff that Red may well retail them on the street, throwing them out for the pleasure of his friends, all of them implacably taking their places in the thoughtfully constructed and disingenuous misogyny of our era. But Red will omit details that subtly link these adventures, that transmute their essential natures, that make them into a single bundle of confused grotesquerie. Red says that *this* is what *happened*.

All right?

Jesus Christ! He asks if maybe people want blood!

Red blunders into the bathroom one day after school and is alarmed and astonished to find Mother standing on the bath mat, naked. Her arms are raised and she is drying her hair with a bath towel that falls in front of her face. For a moment, Red thinks that he may be able to leave without being detected, that Mother will be able to continue her strange womanly rituals in

ignorance of his presence. But Mother sees Red at almost the pre-
cise moment that he freezes at the threshold. He stares at her, his
mouth slack, his hands awkwardly rigid at his sides. Mother
gasps and says that he'd better get, better get, get out of there,
and with her left hand, palm outward, makes a vague, pushing
gesture of rejection. With her other hand she flails at Red with
the towel and then, after he turns and leaves, holds the towel in
front of her body. Later, she says nothing to Red and he pretends
a perfect amnesia. Of course, he remembers her startled, girlish
glance, her lithe arms above her head, her small breasts pulled
taut, her slightly spread legs and between them the darkness
which he has seen without seeing. This image returns again and
again and he's certain that he's turning into a crazy degenerate,
thinking about his own *Mother*! About her naked, about her
thing. He feels like Whitey or Pulciver, some kind of a sex maniac
moron who says he'd like to do it, shit, yeah, with his mother.

Some few days later, Red is poking through Grandpa's
dresser drawer looking for a cheap cardboard telescope that
Father gave him and that was immediately confiscated for God
knows what reason by Grandma, who, as usual, implicated
Grandpa by insisting that he keep the pitiful drunk's cheap
guilt-present, bought without a moment's thought or care, the
slob got it out of a Crackerjack box if truth be told, in his
drawer. Grandma and Mother are on the roof, where
Grandma is supervising Mother's hanging of the wash. Red is
as careful as possible not to disturb the drawer's contents, and
goes by feel rather than sight. He brushes something that feels
like cardboard, a kind of smooth, coated cardboard, and gingerly slides out a photograph.

In a kind of small park or formal garden a wooden bench
occupies the central area of the photograph. On the bench sit
two elaborately moustachioed men, their identical coiffures
shining with pomade and parted severely in the middle. Both

are naked save for black, neatly gartered socks, and sprawled across their thighs is a rather hefty woman, dressed in nothing but black silk stockings rolled and gartered above the knee, and side-buttoned black kid shoes. The men's faces are rather placid, almost complacent, whereas the woman's face is distorted by a large erect penis that fills her mouth and that obviously belongs to the man who is looking at the back of her head benignly. The other man's penis may well be inserted into the woman's vagina, but the angle of the recording camera is such that this cannot be determined. Red trembles as he looks at this adventure, his legs feel weak, and a kind of wonderful nausea grips his stomach and guts. He cannot take his eyes off the woman's greedy mouth.

The front door slams and Red hears Grandma's shuffling steps coming down the hall. He slips the photograph back and slides the drawer closed, but there is no time to get out of the bedroom: there's Grandma. She looks at Red in suspicious, astonished surprise, and he shrugs, fatuously, flushed, and starts slowly toward her and the door, trying out a vapid smile, thinking vainly of some excuse, some reason, but there is no reason for him to be in the bedroom. Grandma likes to say that if you keep your eyes and hands to yourself you might not starve to death. As Red is but a step from Grandma she stops him with a finger to his chest, shaking her head, done up in a black hairnet. She says that although she knows that Red is a treacherous little cur she always got down on her hands and knees to God Almighty and the Pope to pray that he'd escape the curse of the morphoditish blood and impure degeneracy that unfortunately runs in his veins from his Father. Red is ice cold and cannot think how Grandma knows what he has done. She grabs him and turns him around to face the bedroom and says that he's well on his way to a locked ward in Kings County, that he should look, look! beJesus Christ, is he not scarlet with shame? There on the floor, knocked down by accident, perhaps in an excess of clumsiness or excitement on Red's part, sprawls Grandma's corset. Grandma pinches Red's ear with her fingernails as she yanks a belt out of a drawer. She says that it's a true sign of moronic idiocy when a boy who should be out earning a penny or playing in the fresh air with normal boys lolls around the house playing instead with ladies' underwear, probably prancing in front of the mirror with it and imagining God knows what filth! She says that she does not even want to think what the drooling mongolian is up to with his Mother's things! With this, she begins to lash Red's legs, buttocks, thighs, belly, and groin, all the while holding on to his ear, now explosively aflame with agony.

In Red's mind images proffer themselves, shift into and out of focus, substitute for each other, combine in more ways that Red can follow: Father and Grandfather naked on the couch with Mother: Red and Grandma naked in the bathroom: Red wearing Grandma's corset looking at Mother and another Red on a bench with a towel across their bare thighs: everything shifts and splinters, is reconfigured in claustrophobic kaleidoscopic distortion: Mother's mouth distended as she drinks thirstily from Grandpa's bottle of Wilson's: Mother in her underpants, a towel on her head, while Grandpa chats with a naked Mr. Svensen: and: and. Red has a terrible, painful erection that seems to want to pull itself free of his body and that gets harder, that feels as if it will split open as Grandma whips him furiously, occasionally landing a blow directly to his straining penis, taking Red's breath away in a near faint. Red's eyes swim wildly in his head, he is lost, blind, drowning in a black sea of fire as his pelvis begins to jerk spasmodically and his knees buckle in orgasm. Grandma lashes on in silent rage, fueled by his stupid, drooling smile. She starts whacking his head as he sinks to the floor, the pig!

Red may retail these narratives on the street, but he will omit the details that attenuate their surfaces. Only Red knows the true narratives and because they are so confused in their being, so incapable of being segregated, Red himself does not know all. Although it may be his Mother surprised naked, Jesus Christ!, his Grandpa's dirty picture, Holy God Almighty!, his Grandma mistaking his excitement for a stranger excitement and beating the shit out of him, God damn it!, all will be tamed, all surfaces smoothed, all made to conform to the invented eroticism which conceals Red's nameless pleasure.

FORTY SIX

❖

Red walks through the park in the cold wind and blowing leaves of another grey day: restless and sad, morose and lonely. There is a smell of rain in the air and Red watches a couple of little kids, in hilarious embrace, roll over and over down the bare hill, the dumb little bastards! Alone, alone, he feels as if he might like to cry. He pulls a crumpled cigarette out of his shirt pocket and lights it with a wooden match that he ignites with his thumbnail, something he's mastered to show the other guys what's what. But this expertise cannot alleviate the smothering pity he feels for himself in his isolate sadness.

What does anything matter? Red is alone and miserable, the rotting world has set itself against him as have the wind, the grey skies, the emptiness of the dingy park. People can go crazy from weather like this, it's a fact that was in "Ripley's Believe It or Not." Especially kids can go crazy, they call it nervous prostration that happens on account of different worries, one day a kid is all right and the next day he's prostrative. It can also happen because of girls, liking girls and being sad because of liking girls, and also whacking off too much because of thinking of girls, the little hooers.

Red heads slowly toward a clump of bushes in the most remote area of the park, the crest of a little hill that overlooks the grey, choppy waters of the Narrows: the bushes where he took Patsy. Red takes a deep drag on his Old Gold and feels the wind pull a couple of delicious tears backward across his pimply cheeks. O Patsy, Patsy. Red says, into the wind, that Patsy is a beautiful saint of a girl, then he tries a sob and takes another drag on his cigarette, a little bit like George Raft in a nightclub in one of those rich-guy white jackets.

Patsy. The way she, Jesus Christ, sat with her legs open.

Red shoulders his way into the dense bushes and sits down precisely in the spot where he and Patsy sat, and kissed, and where she became his girlfriend, right? Red whispers that he *wants* Patsy, he wants her to be his girlfriend, he can't stand it that she doesn't want to see him anymore or even take a walk with him to the park to eat some candy and talk about school and Patsy's dreams of chatting with the Virgin Mary and also of going to Fontbonne Hall with the rich stuck-up girls from Ridge Boulevard and Colonial Road like Joanne Carman. She doesn't want anything to do with Red. She says that she hates him. Red looks up at the sky and closes his eyes. Alone and sad. His round shoulders heave with his pitiful groans.

Red says, to God, that he doesn't know, not actually, really, why Patsy is so mad at him, he only wants to be her boyfriend and pick flowers for her, when available. Maybe save up for or steal a Duncan quarter yo-yo.

Patsy showed her underwear to Red and she liked showing it and now she says that she hates him and her dumb slob of a mother gives him the fish eye, the fat-assed bitch. Red isn't Big Mickey or somebody, for Christ's sake, or some weird bastard like Hips Ticino slowly pulling a raw frankfurter out of his open fly right in class last week so that Miss Crane almost had a stroke, now *there* is a real hoople.

Patsy should have known he was only kidding when he said he'd say what he said he'd say, he'd never say to anybody what he said to her he'd say. Never. She should have known he was just nervous.

Alone in the cold park, alone alone in the cold. Red pretends that Patsy will suddenly stick her grimy bucktoothed weasel face through the bushes and smile at him, but she's not coming, she's just another God damned bitch like all girls, making a mountain out of a molehill, Jesus Christ, he didn't actually really hump her, he just sort of poked it into her a little and came all over the place. It's not anything to get excited about. Red considers that maybe it was *sort* of a hump but he didn't have a cundrum on like a man or anything. She opened her legs all by herself, she wanted to, the Virgin Mary could take a walk for Herself that day, Patsy knew that his secret word was a lot of horseshit, she just went right along with the gag. Now poor Red has to suffer for giving a girl what she wanted.

Will nobody ever care for Red and his crooked green teeth, his coarse red hair, his big feet, chapped hands, and black, broken fingernails? Is he not the very salt of the earth? Why must he be so alone when the girl he kind of likes, a little, in a respectable Catholic-boy way, really, it's not like they're a couple of Protestants that don't have God right there in church in the vigil light looking down at everybody all the time, and likes even more when she skips rope every day right after school in front of her house acts like he's not even alive? With her plaid skirt flying up like she has no idea what she's showing to everybody.

Red suddenly begins to cry in wondrous, amazed earnest as a spatter of rain rattles among the bushes. He is thinking of sticking it into Patsy's little box, how nice it felt. He is thinking of how maybe he could have got her to do some other dirty things if he hadn't been such a palooka. Nobody loves him!

The rain starts to come down steadily and Red crawls out of his hiding place to make a dash for the doorway of the parky's tool shack. They say the parky takes girls in there. Red turns and looks at the bushes and grimaces. How sad he feels because of the raw deal he's been handed.

As he starts to run for the shack he is struck by his stupidity in not staying on the good side of that spoiled little snot, Nancy O'Neill, shit! He could maybe probably have got *her* into the bushes with him, she's a born tramp, maybe he still can.

No. He can't. Nobody likes Red. And all he wants is to give these two bitches what they want and they stick their noses up at him.

Red pants out, in ragged puffs of thin vapor, that he hopes they both get the clapp-siff, if, as Grandma says, God is good.

FORTY SEVEN

❖

Red sits at the kitchen table, staring out of the abyss of his ignorance at a page of fraction exercises in his arithmetic textbook, when Grandma, with the well-timed abruptness that even Red has never been able to get used to, says that she's got to have some vinegar for the navy beans, that Grandpa has got to have vinegar on his beans or the poor man will have a face on him down to the floor, it's well known that he can be a real pill about such things. She says that she wants Red to run to the store *now*, he'll have plenty of time later to do his homework, much good it will do him! the lout of a boy will be fortunate indeed if he turns out to be a street sweeper. Grandma reaches for her purse.

Red looks up from the mysterious page and says that he won't go to the store. His heart feels as if it is about to fill his chest and cut off his breath, and his ears are burning. He waits for the blow across the back of his neck from the spatula in Grandma's hand. In the silence, there is only the soft popping sound of the navy beans simmering on the stove.

Grandma says that she *thinks* that she just told Red to go around the corner to the kraut and buy a bottle of vinegar. She says that she has the notion, she must be losing her mind, she must be hearing things, she may be dreaming, but she has the idea that Red said that he would *not* go to the store? This can't be the case, it's too snot-nosed brazen even for a disobedient, selfish pup like Red. Grandma says that it's getting very close to suppertime, that she'll want the vinegar right away now, that Red is to stop all this rigmarole and *run*. Red closes his book, looks at Grandma, and says again that he will not go to the store, that he doesn't want to go to the store, that he's tired of being sent everywhere for things whenever Grandma feels like it. He lifts his eyes and sees Grandma's pale face and stunned expression, and immediately looks down at the floor. He's just about to say that he's sorry that he can't go but thinks better of it. Grandma is going to torture him whether he's sorry or not, and as of this minute, for him to change his mind, beg forgiveness, and dash out to the store would in no measure obviate or lessen the punishment that Grandma is, doubtlessly, even now devising. Let it be.

O Jesus Christ, let it fall on him once and for all.

Red sits, tense, waiting, his eyes screwed into slits in preparation for the violent pain that will force them closed. But there is no pain, only a dreadful silence.

Grandma sets down the spatula and crosses to the kitchen door, where, in a perfectly modulated weak version of her girlish falsetto says that by Jesus Himself, the Son of God, in His three hours of agony on the Cross, she never thought that she would live to see the black day when her own grandson, a boy she cherishes despite his ingratitude and degenerated ways, when this terrible boy would defy her to her face in her own house, never. *Never*. Mother and Grandpa are the addressees of these stunned, heartbroken, and pitiable remarks, and enter the kitchen where they are told the unbelievable story. Grandma positions herself behind them as they stand over Red, and makes a noise, some kind of a noise. Red, in horror, realizes that she is whimpering? She's whimpering!

Jesus H. Fucking Christ.

Mother says that Red really should. Grandpa wonders who Red thinks he is. Mother says that we all have our tasks. Grandpa says work and fingers and bone and nigger and roof and head and food and table. Mother says it's not a lot to and that everybody has a cross. Grandpa says table and food and head and roof and nigger and bone and fingers and work. Grandma whimpers, occasionally saying Jesus Christ and sweet pure Mary and the host of Angels and who would have dreamed that. A boy. A boy! She whimpers.

Red stares vapidly at his Mother's feet and then at Grandpa's feet and says that he'll go to the store for vinegar or for anything else if Mother tells him to go to the store, or if Grandpa tells him to go to the store. But he won't go to the store for Grandma, he won't, he can't explain it. There's no use talking about it, he just won't go to the store. For Grandma. He looks up at them. Grandpa's expression is identical to the one he wears when he wants to sneak his bottle of Wilson's into the bathroom for a couple of swallows, and Mother's is that of someone straining to move her bowels. Grandma, who is partially concealed behind Mother, has fallen silent.

It is unthinkable that either Grandpa or Mother will tell Red to go to the store. Red knows this to be the case, as does Grandma, and both know that the other knows. For a strange moment, the kitchen is home to a silent electricity of conspiracy between Red and Grandma, one that holds both Grandpa and Mother in contempt. He almost wants to push Mother aside so that he can look into Grandma's face to discover the scorn there. Mother says that it's not her place to send Red anywhere, that Grandma is cooking, that Grandma needs what she needs and there's no two ways about it, that Mother would expect Red to go out to the store for her if she needed something, certainly, and that Grandma has the right to expect, the right to expect that, and who in hell does Red think he is anyway? She dutifully and cravenly slaps him across the face, and Red imagines the twitch of Grandma's little smile. Grandpa says that that's the way he feels, absolutely, one hundred per cent. He agrees with every word that Mother says, and with Grandma too, of course, and he can't fathom what Red thinks he's doing up on his high horse and Grandpa would not, no, not for a king's ransom, ask Red to go anywhere! For, as Mother says. And Mother is Mother. Grandpa says, finally, that all this fuss over vinegar is, well, all this fuss over *vinegar*, and he doesn't even *need* vinegar on his beans.

There is a brief, confused milling about and then Mother sets the table, Grandma, sniffling a little, starts frying chuck chopped and onions, and supper, as always, approaches, is consumed, and ends in shards of spiritless conversation. Red's astonishing disobedience is, astonishingly, not mentioned again, and Grandma makes no move to punish him. On the contrary, she speaks to him, when she must, with an obvious softening of her wonted tone.

Can it be possible that Red's self-assertiveness has somehow tempered Grandma's disdain and contumely, scorn and contempt?

No. Red knows. No.

The next morning, Grandma asks Red if he'd like a couple of fried eggs for breakfast, an unheard-of offer. He expresses no surprise, and says, casually, that eggs would be fine. Grandma does not offer eggs to Mother or Grandpa and they scrupulously make nothing of this. The entire scene is oddly unbalanced, aberrant.

On his way to school, Red thinks everything over, and comes—easily, easily—to the belief, the certainty, rather, that Grandma is making certain that Red's insurrection will be bounded by instances of the unusual: she does not want Red to forget, or even to diminish the memory of, his refusal. She wants it to stand forth, she wants him to remember, with glassy clarity, his saying *no* to her.

No. To Grandma. *No.* Red said *no* to Grandma!

Red considers the smile that Grandma flashed at him as she served the eggs, a smile so meticulously engineered to conceal malice and the desire to injure that its very false candor exuded the malicious and injurious. But Red knows that only he saw this and that Mother and Grandpa saw what they stupidly took to be a sign of the amelioration of—of what? Of everything.

Red says ha ha. And again, ha ha. He says bullshit.

He shuffles and scuffs and dawdles on toward school, knowing that although nothing has improved, something has changed. Knowing, too, that Grandma is planning something for Red that will probably amaze even her with its laboriously petty cruelty. His reply to this certain misery impending is to kick over a full, reeking garbage can and say, his rotten teeth clenched, his dim psyche in forever-irreparable fragments, that Grandma can take it right up her fat nose.

FORTY EIGHT

❖

Weeks have passed since the enormity of Red's refusal, and although Grandma insults, batters, and whips Red as usual, she has inflicted no extraordinary punishment on him, nothing that Red has decided will be drastic enough for God to send her to a torture chamber for life, and then to roast in Hell, covered from head to foot with eternally blazing cockroaches. Red despises and fears her secret, dark powers more than ever, yet he tries to compose his blurry features into an expression of blasé indifference or icily bitter contempt. Grandma casually disturbs these inadequate masks with sudden rabbit punches and elbow thrusts to the ribs. She shakes her head and says that he is nothing but a whipped mongrel.

It's a cold day, and Red bumps into Father, half-drunk and with an extraordinarily colorful facial bruise in sickening tones of orange, red, blue, and purple, that extends from his cheekbone up to his hairline. He's on the corner, a soggy Sigaro di Nobile smoldering in his mouth, his hands in the ripped pockets of a greenish-black benny. Red feels like pushing him into the gutter and jumping on him or yelling, but when Father smiles at him, wincing, Red stands there in dumb despair. Father puts an arm around his shoulders and they walk down the street and enter Hellberg's, an ice-cream parlor that Father sweeps and mops every morning for coffee and cake and a quarter. He says that what the hell, somebody's got to do the nigger work, beggars can't be choosers, when a guy is down on his luck he's down on his luck. Father leans over the fountain counter to say something to old Hellberg in a soft voice, then turns to Red and they walk into the back room.

A couple of fifteen-year-old girls in soft pink crewneck sweaters against which the collars of their white blouses lie so crisply and modestly that Red feels like busting them in the face are drinking cokes at a table near the jukebox. They watch Red and Father openly as they sit down, then look at each other, theatrically wide-eyed, and giggle behind their hands. Red wonders what they'd do if he walked over there and pissed in their cokes, the stuck-up twats.

Jesus Christ, his Father is a real bum, a *bum*.

Father says something about a good day for hot chocolate, and then is up to go to the fountain and return in a few seconds with two hot chocolates with whipped cream, and Social Teas on the saucers. The girls make funny faces at each other and Red hopes that the little hooers get the clap from Hellberg's toilet seat because the old bastard's got it, so they say.

Father asks Red how things are, and says that things with him are not so jake, that Margie, his, well, Red knows, his wife, sort of asked him to take a powder for a while. Her old man, her first old man, Terry's father, decided to stay ashore for a while, got tired of shipping out all the time, and they sort of talked things over, and, well. Father smiles and shrugs and lights a Twenty Grand, then offers the pack to Red, who doesn't bat an eye as he takes a cigarette, then leans into

Father's proffered light. The dumb sluts can stare till their eyes
fall out.

Father says that he never really much liked Terry anyway, a
sneaky sort of a kid, a kid who's always got an angle or a
dodge, he's a bad apple, he's about Red's age and he's already
trying to take advantage of girls if Red knows what, well, he'll
know when he's a little older. On the other hand, Father says
that Margie is a hell of a good skate, Red would love her if he
got to know her, she likes to take a drink, have a laugh or two,
play a little gin and casino and hearts, not a damn thing high
hat about the woman. Dances like a dream. Knows the words
to all the old songs and lots of the new ones too. Well. He says
that when the sailors come back from the sea and the hunters
in from the woods, like in the poem, well. Women have to do
things they ordinarily wouldn't do or maybe wouldn't even
want to do. He says that people talk. Father sighs and carefully
takes a pint of Dixie Belle gin out of his pocket and just as carefully pours a couple of inches into what's left of his hot chocolate. He says that of course he had a little talk with the man,
Joe, Joe Walsh is his name, a chief electrician, they had a face-
to-face talk, and Father says that he tried to tell him how much
he respected Margie, what a swell girl she is, and she didn't
know whether Joe was dead or alive, really. A hell of a nice girl,
never a dull moment with good old Margie. And Terry too,
when all is said and done, Terry too, God bless the kid. He says
that Joe just could not see it any way but his own, ah well, ah
well, he says that Joe got a little salty, he'd had a drink, and,
well. Seamen. Father asks how things are with him and Mother
and the old bitch, pardon his French, witch, and Caspar Mil-
quetoast.

Red says that Grandma is worse than ever and that Mother
sticks up for her most of the time, that if Grandma hits him,
Mother hits him too, and if Grandma just yells at him, Mother

hits him anyway. She makes up for Grandma, it's terrible, he doesn't know how he can stand it, he can't wait to join the Marines. The girls get up to leave and Red takes a deep drag on his cigarette and blows the smoke toward them, his eyes narrowed. Maybe he'll just walk over there and grab their little tits for them.

Father says that Mother has to do. She and Grandma and Grandpa have. It's. The old woman and when Mother was. No better than a nance with the pretzels he takes. Red is not to worry. Every dog will have and the world is his oyster. If Father knew what was in store. No need for Joe Walsh. A hell of a nice woman. No reason to blame Mother. No. No. A saint. Some day when he's a little older he'll.

Red accepts another cigarette and sees that Father's face is wet with tears, but he is not only unmoved and unimpressed, he feels a vague disgust. Red is especially tired of hearing him talk about how wonderful Mother is, wonderful, shit, another bitch like Grandma and Margie Walsh and all the rest of them. Miss O'Reilly. Father lights Red's cigarette and pours some more gin into his cup, then lifts it in a burlesque toast. He says that there's no harm in having a drink once in a while, might as well be hanged for a sheep as a goat or a lamb or whatever it is. He says that Red should put all his hurt feelings aside and obey his Mother, God knows, and love her, God knows that *he* still loves her after all that's happened and if it hadn't been for a couple of little slips she made that anybody could make and on the spur of the moment, well. He says that she's only flesh and blood. He says that Christ knows he's no saint and that he made a couple of mistakes himself, temptation can be a terrible thing, but let somebody else throw the first stone cast at the glass house, that's what he's always believed. He swallows his gin.

The room is growing dim in the waning afternoon, and only

the glowing jukebox casts its pale orange light on the tile floor and marble tabletops. Red is getting a very bad feeling listening to Father talk about mistakes and temptation. There's a strange darkness hovering around his mumbles and slurring that Red is afraid will suddenly blaze into light and reveal something that Red does not want to see. Father leans back in his chair and a thin stench of sweat and booze slides into Red's nose. Father says that life is hard and that's what life is but that a man can only do his best. Jesus Christ, he's doing his best and next week he's going down to the Navy Yard or Erie Basin where they're hiring for defense, lay off the sauce, make some real money hand over fist with the OT they're handing out. He says that he knows that Red needs things.

Red feels like going outside and leaving this piss-assed drunk alone with his gin and his bullshit. He could jump in front of a truck and that would be that, or he could go down to the pier and just fall into the water, let the tide take him out to the ocean so that they'd never find him, the fucking fuck fucks.

He bends down and pretends to tie his shoe so that Father can't see his face, not that he gives a damn because it just doesn't matter. This is how the world is. Grandma doesn't love Grandpa, Grandpa doesn't love Grandma, neither of them love Mother, Mother doesn't love them, Father is a drunken slob and doesn't love Mother or Grandma or Grandpa or Margie Walsh or Terry or Joe, and they don't love him, and none of them love Red and Red doesn't give a shit. Red hates the whole God damn world. He straightens up and asks Father for another smoke and how about a sip of that gin. He wishes to Christ that he could, that he could, that he could what? He thinks to reach over and touch his father's thick useless hand. No soap.

FORTY NINE

❖

For a long time, Red believes Mother when she says that all his baby pictures were carried off by Father without her knowledge, but one day he realizes that there were never any baby pictures of him, that she is lying. Like the rest of them.

One day Miss Crane, her eyes rolling and bleary and her slip hanging well below the hem of her wrinkled dress, gets up shakily from her desk and, off balance, begins writing on the blackboard with her fountain pen. Big Mickey throws and hits her with a tomato-and-mayonnaise sandwich, Whitey with an apple, and Sal Rongo with a chalky eraser. As she begins to cry, Red, almost hysterically elated by the smell of helplessness, loses control of himself and pisses his pants.

Red reads in *Know the MEANING of Your DREAMS* in the five-and-ten that a dream of finding paper money in an empty room or house means that serious illness, and perhaps death, will strike someone near and dear. That evening, he mentions that he had such a dream the night before and is pleased to see Grandma pale for that brief moment before she sees directly into his mind.

When Miss O'Reilly leans with her thighs against the edge of her desk, while reading or talking to the class, her garter clasps make small bumps in the taut fabric of her skirt, driving Red to utter distraction by this awesome proof of her actual womanhood. This truth causes him to masturbate so frequently and obsessively that he turns ash grey, his eyes cross with fatigue, and he falls asleep every night at the supper table; from which impromptu naps Grandma awakens him by light blows to the head with the sugar bowl.

Often, just before sleep, Red sees Grandma's gold tooth gleaming in the perpetual twilight of the long hallway as she opens her mouth to destroy him: bitch, gorgon, harpy, goon.

The thick sheaf of letters, bound together by a heavy rubber band, are all addressed to Grandma in Father's hand. Red holds them, his eyes narrowing, Red holds them, his eyes closing.

Pushed beyond all patience, and unable to muster even one more shred of required self-degradation, Red smacks Big Mickey across the head with a slat from an orange crate. As he sees blood start from his victim's mouth, a quick splotch of the most startling crimson, he realizes that to hurt things is to stop being afraid. How is it that this has never before come so clear to him?

Some photographs taken at Far Rockaway before Red was born show Grandma and Grandpa, Grandpa and Father, Grandma and Father, Grandma and Grandpa and Father, an unidentified woman and Father, cousin Katy and Grandpa and Father, another unidentified woman and an unidentified man and Grandma and Father, and Father and a Studebaker coupe. Where was Mother on that bright day?

Grandma says that as Jesus Christ was killed by the Jews it's not from *her* side of the family that Red's hair comes, no indeed, that color is the sure sign of shanty riffraff who sleep with the pigs and chickens.

Red is sent to the Principal's office after he and Pulciver

steal a substitute teacher's lunch and attendance book. When the Principal asks him what his Mother and Father are going to say about his terrible conduct, Red says that they were both killed when they fell off the roof. Last week. He tries to cry, but instead, blows snot all over his shirt.

Whitey buys Red a baloney and potato salad sandwich on a hard roll, and a Pepsi, then offers him a Camel from a full pack. Red says thanks, and they smoke for a while before Whitey says that he's got plenty of money left from the deuce that some old guy in the park gave him to give Whitey a blow job. Red nods wisely, then chuckles, wondering what a blow job is.

Red is beginning to lose all sense of his true inclinations, and to confuse one thing with another, for one of his defenses against Grandma's diverse assaults is to pretend to like that which he dislikes, and dislike that which he likes. He is also vacantly opinionless about virtually everything so as to confuse, even momentarily, Grandma's mental inventory of his weaknesses.

One evening at supper, when Grandma is suggesting to Mother that Father is and has always been a deadbeat syphilitic morphodite who should have been, God forgive her, stillborn, she turns, amazingly, to ask Red what *he* thinks of his bum of a Father. Red, hopelessly unprepared, says that he thinks that people should honor thy father and thy mother, and Grandma, after looking at him with a kind of distant pity, throws a bowl of stewed tomatoes in his face.

Sometimes Red hears Mother crying in the bathroom, the only place, she says, that she can have any privacy at all. At such times he wishes that she would marry the fat bookie who stands on the subway corner, or the cab driver with the shakes, or the bald counterman in the diner, or Phil the butcher, even though he's a kike and looks at her in a way that makes Red feel as if his stomach is going to turn over.

The new teacher of the release-time catechism class is Sister Theresa, a young, pale nun with a thin, delicate nose and grey eyes. When she first speaks of the terrible sins of impurity in thought and deed, and of how they truly make God weep, a faint pink blush colors the flesh over her cheekbones, and Red falls in love.

Red holds one of Grandpa's Gillette single-edge razor blades over one of his wrists and wonders how long it takes for all the blood to run out of somebody Grandma's size.

Red filches one cigarette daily from Grandpa's pack of Luckies, and one day is pleased and shocked, in equal measure, to discover that Grandpa knows this and has known it from the beginning. He feels bad but not bad enough to stop stealing, because Grandpa is a God damn mollycoddle.

Sal Rongo says to Red that the idea of heaven and hell is a lot of bullshit since how come priests don't want to die any more than any other dumb cluck, and Big Mickey says that Sal is so fucking stupid that it's a fucking wonder that he can even fucking walk. Red edges away because he knows that when Sal and Mickey quarrel, other people get hurt.

Father buys Red a barbecue sandwich and a glass of milk in the Surprise one day and tells him that he wants him to know that he always did right by Mother and that she should have stuck by him, that he worshiped the ground that Mother walked on and that she should have stuck it, for Christ's sake, out, that he still has the greatest respect for Mother, and he doesn't understand why she won't even let him take her out for a cup of coffee and talk to her. He sniffles and lights a cigarette, and to the counterman's query as to how the world is treating him replies that he can't complain.

Red wonders how it feels to wear a vest, a two-way-stretch girdle, a tuxedo, step-ins, a Homburg, a corset, a monocle, silk stockings, a polo coat, foxtails, a cravat, high heels, spectators, a slip, a moustache, lipstick, a tie clasp, a brassiere, and a dozen other things that testify to authentic adulthood. When he looks at his awkward sack of a body in Grandma's closet-door mirror, he spits on the glass.

In the Confessional, Red says that he hates his Grandma because she yells at him and whips him and beats him all the time, and the priest says that he must do his best to stop trying the poor woman's patience, that grandmothers haven't got the strength of a young fellow, that children must be understanding of the old. Red adds that he wishes that she would die in a really horrible way, like maybe being cut in half by a trolley car. There is a long silence from the other side of the grille.

Grandma says that she's found out for sure that cousin Katy has cancer and that she's not long for this world, the poor thing. Her voice breaks and she takes a yellow-crusted handkerchief out of her housedress pocket to wipe her eyes. Red fears that he's going to laugh at this disgusting play.

One day, alone in the apartment, Red unaccountably begins to whip his bare legs, his back, and his chest with Grandma's belt. As he lashes himself harder, sweat pouring down his flushed face, he becomes uncontrollably excited and aroused. Still flogging himself, he undoes, shamefully, the buttons of his fly.

Red is told by Grandma and Mother that he cannot join the Boy Scouts and that it doesn't matter what Kicky's mother and Bubbsy's mother let *them* do, because everybody knows that the God damn Boy Scouts are all some class of crazy Protestants, full of pimples and smelling of cod-liver oil, and working night and day to make Catholic boys renounce their faith.

Margie sends Red a belated birthday card on which she has written, "Sorry to be so late, your Friend, Margie," and Mother and Grandma take turns screaming at him and slapping his face red and swollen.

Red sees Whitey taking a nine-year-old girl into the cellar of a building down the street, and for a moment thinks that maybe he ought to tell somebody about Whitey. But then he thinks it's none of his business, the kid knows what she's doing, and besides, Whitey is O.K.

Red and everybody else is astonished when a girl named Ruthie is introduced to the boys as a new member of 6A-4. Before the day is over they realize that if Ruthie belongs anywhere, she belongs right there, because when Sal Rongo asks her if she ever fucking heard of soap and water she tells him that he can suck her pussy.

Red is plunged into misery when it occurs to him that photographs of Grandma, taken when she was young, show clearly that she looked then almost exactly the way Mother looks now.

The corpse of a rabid dog, shot by a cop on the corner of the Cities Service station, looks to Red so remarkably peaceful that even the shining flies clustered and buzzing on his bloody head cannot dispel the sense of calm surrounding him, the stillness, the repose, the hush.

On a photograph of Grandma standing beneath a tree, smiling yet severe in a fur coat and cloche, Red, in careful letters, writes DIRTY OLD CUNT. He props the photograph against the sugar bowl on the kitchen table, and goes in to sit on the couch, to wait quietly for Grandma and Mother. Ecstatic, he feels the world on the edge of obliteration.